#epicschoolprank

Quineka Ragsdale

Unfortunate circumstances may affect you, but don't let them become you

1 D'ANTHONY MCGEE

The cheerleaders didn't look half bad, D'Anthony thought. Too bad they were wearing the wrong color. He was wearing the wrong color too, black and gray, but he was on the right team, although he was sitting on the wrong side. He had just watched his team dominate the first half and he was excited to take part in the epic finale.

D'Anthony stood in the bleachers. Near the stairs, close enough to see the halftime show. He knew he wouldn't stay long. Soon enough, the sound of the panther would remind him of his mission. He had to be at the designated spot at the exact time.

"Hey man… where'd you get that knock off?" A fat guy and a lanky dude in a black letterman laughed as they were leaving the bleachers. The round one had a face like a duck and the long one had a face like a turtle. The Huey P. Newton Panthers produced some funny looking guys. D'Anthony instinctively rubbed his hand down the back of his fade. They eyed his shirt as they walked past. D'Anthony looked down at his clothes. He didn't know what the big deal was. He wore black and gray like everyone else in the stands.

The crowd roared. D'Anthony's head whipped toward the field. The Panther's mascot pranced across the front of the band in a rhythmic motion. Brass overtook the woodwind, followed by the percussions drowning them all. The crowd sang along to what had to be their stupid school song. He laughed as he thought about the mighty black and gray being covered in blue, yellow and red.

The panther mascot urged someone to the field. Someone that D'Anthony couldn't see. Whatever it was, it caused the entire crowd to laugh. He looked around until the other person came into view. It was a rapture. The person in the costume was much taller than usual, but he wore the same colors D'Anthony would have worn if he wasn't in stealth mode. It seemed the Huey P. Newton Panthers had a prank up their sleeves too. He wondered if the football team knew that their mascot was missing. If they did, no one told him about it. This must've happened right before the game. Or after the party the night before.

The brass band took center stage as the music made a dramatic turn. D'Anthony watched as his school's mascot walked around with his head down. Apparently, he was upset that he couldn't dance and move as well as the clumsy black cat. D'Anthony couldn't stop his face from turning into a scowl. They were making a mockery of his school.

The panther mascot had a solution to the falcon's problem. He pulled out a Panther jersey just like the one he wore and offered it to the

Heru mascot. Elated, the falcon angrily ripped off his jersey and threw it on the field. He took the Panther jersey and put it on. The percussions took center stage again as the brass and woodwinds complemented the upbeat tempo. The crowd almost drowned the band when the familiar tune of local rapper, Big Weight's national hit, Do it For Ya Boy began to play. Suddenly, the mascot was able to do the same dance and routine as the panther. The Panther dancers, cheerleaders and band joined in the same stupid dance.

Faint boos could barely be heard from the other side of the field. The panther pumped his fist as they chanted, *Power to the People, Power to the Panthers,* over and over again. Even the Heru falcon joined in pumping his fist to the chant. D'Anthony could see security officers stopping anyone from the Heru side from running onto the field. A panther had the microphone. "Uh oh," a male voice yelled, "looks like someone wishes they were a panther." No one on the panther's side was seated. Each passing second they jumped higher and yelled louder. If D'Anthony wasn't afraid that it would ruin Chey's whole plan, he would have run out onto the field himself and forced their mascot to take off that ugly jersey. He could imagine Chey squealing about him ruining the plan. But how would that look anyway? He had on the same colors.

The cheerleaders, dancers and band parted the middle of the field for the mascots to walk through. Both mascots stopped walking to hold the Heru jersey in the air. Each side of the walkway leaned back as far as they could before leaning forward all at once. A huge spit sound came over the loudspeaker as the entire field seemed to spit on the Heru jersey. The mascots threw the jersey on the ground, stomped it, then continued down their path. The cheerleaders, dancers and band began to seal the walkway behind them as they ended their walk in front of the Heru bleachers. The music stopped as the entire field chanted again, ending with their fists in the air.

The Heru bleachers threw whatever they could find toward the field as the band and mascots dispersed. *Don't worry falcons, revenge is coming soon enough,* D'Anthony thought. He barely heard that ugly cat snarl from his phone. He turned the alarm sound off as he sped down the steps. He didn't need to see the third quarter. He had a mission to complete.

He felt like he could finally breathe once he was outside of the fence. It felt weird being behind enemy lines. "Bruh, where'd you get that shirt?" He heard someone question him, but he kept walking. After that halftime show, he was focused more than ever. He had plenty of time to do the two minute walk, but he didn't want time to get sidetracked. Chey nagged and nagged that if anything went wrong, it would be D'Anthony's fault. He would prove him wrong. He had to be waiting and ready for the next wounded panther alarm. He was proud that the alarm sound was his idea.

The closer he got to the front of the school, the more he saw the familiar blue, yellow and red. He kept his head down in case a Falcon noticed him. He noticed a familiar pair of tennis in those custom school colors. He was nervous that he could be spotted.

"You're always trying to burn shit," D'Anthony heard a guy say. He looked over and saw three Panther fans talking with each other. There were two guys and a girl. All wearing black and gray.

Shit. D'Anthony finally realized his mistake. Panthers wore black and gray. What he had on was not the same. He wore gray and black. The colors were the same, but not in the same place. D'Anthony didn't think it was a big deal, but he knew that Chey would. He always cared about the details. Details no one would even notice. Except apparently some stupid panthers.

"What's up girl," D'Anthony looked up to see his middle school crush. He stopped flirting with her when she got with one of the basketball players. The owner of those blue, yellow and red kicks he had just passed. He didn't understand why they even dated. She was way too smart for him. Her pinched eyebrows and angry scowl was a stark contrast to her lovely heart shaped face. She didn't even look his way. He watched her extremely long, school colored braids sway from side to side. Her eyes were glued straight ahead. In the direction D'Anthony had just come from. That was probably a good thing. He didn't want to miss a moment because, if she stopped to talk to him, he would have had to make time. Damn. He forgot that fast that he was supposed to be in stealth mode.

He snuck a quick glance at another guy wearing gray and black with the matching hat covering his locs. He pretended to scroll on his phone. D'Anthony paced a bit faster. He didn't want to be the only person not in place. In the front of the panther's raggedy school, he passed by another student in gray and black who pretended to tie his shoelaces. D'Anthony was definitely the only person not where he was supposed to be. He added a little skip to his step. Chey was adamant about them not running. They didn't want to bring attention to themselves. This was a covert operation.

D'Anthony looked around to make sure no one was looking at him. It made sense for the other guys to be early. They had to worry about being seen. There was too much traffic on their sides. D'Anthony got the easiest spot around the school. The other side of the school was the walkway from the game to the parking lot that was in front of the school. The front of the school was, well… the front of the school. His side was nothing. Just a few large bushes and a perfect blind spot. There wasn't even a light near the steel drum that he was looking for.

He walked along the side of the school, a few feet away from the black steel drum. There it was, the small orange cone that told him where the supplies were. He fished his gloves out of his pocket and put each one on carefully. He reached his arm underneath the bushes to find the containers. There were three of them. One by one, he moved each container next to the steel drum, just as he had practiced. The two white containers were to be poured into the drum. The black container would wait on the alarm. D'Anthony didn't know how Chey got everything in position perfectly, but it was just as they had planned.

Seconds then minutes passed before D'Anthony thought to look at his phone. He was nervous. He didn't want to be the one to make a mistake. He didn't want anyone to make a mistake. Especially after that halftime show. They had to do it right and it had to be perfect. He pulled his phone from his pocket just as that annoying cat roared.

"Shit!" He dropped his phone into his pocket quickly as he emptied the black container into the steel drum. He left his evidence as he ran through the darkness to the meetup spot. A borrowed, black sedan sat in the shadows at the edge of the parking lot waiting for him.

D'Anthony thought he heard a loud boom but was sure it was his nerves getting the best of him. He was still nervous. He didn't want to get caught. It wasn't until he made it to the sedan that he realized something went horribly wrong. From where he stood, it seemed the entire school was engulfed in flames.

"Come on man, let's go!" The gray and black shirts caught up with him. He followed their lead into the car. Everyone's heads were turned behind them. Even the driver, Montreal, kept looking through the rearview mirror, "Man, what did y'all do?" Montreal asked.

2 TROY BROWN

The gray and black shirt caught Troy's eye. The guy could be anyone. He only saw the back of his low haircut and black jeans. *Did we change something up,* he wondered. He and Tuck had just laughed at a guy wearing a similar shirt. When he thought about it, it was probably the same guy. He looked around at the other Panther T-shirts. They were like his. Weird. As if that wasn't strange enough, he saw the guy in the weird shirt catch up to two other guys in the same matching shirts. One had long locs falling from a panther cap and the other was in basketball shorts. They disappeared into the parking lot.

The loud boom made Troy jump. By the time he turned to find out what the noise was, something was coming right at him. He turned to run, but it was too late. A heavy object landed right on his calf, stopping his next step short. He fell hard on the pavement. Before he could get his bearings, a sharp pain ripped through his left arm, then another on his right shoulder. Troy balled into the fetal position when he realized he was being trampled. It was getting hot, really fast. He wanted to take off his letterman to help him cool. He questioned everything. *Is this death? Does death burn? Am I going to hell?*

He was being dragged across the courtyard. "No," he started to scream as he began to look around. It was a blue letterman to his left and a black one to his right. Troy was relieved. He wasn't being dragged to hell, he was being saved. The two guys dropped him on a picnic table and ran back toward the commotion.

It was a fire. His school was on fire. It was huge. Everyone was running away from the school. Either toward the parking lot or back to the stadium. The last time Troy saw the game it was 28 - 7. The falcons were cheering just as he left the stadium gates, so Troy was sure they must have scored again. Troy was standing next to his friends, laughing about the halftime show when something stole his attention. He wondered, what happened?

He heard screaming. He hoped no one was hurt, but that's when it hit him. He was hurt. His hand was red. He stood up only to fall back onto the table. Ouch... He pulled his pants leg to find what pained him. The bruise had to have been three shades of purple.

He heard a girl crying and realized a few more people had been dragged to the courtyard.

"What's happening," another girl questioned.

9

"Ay man, you alright?" Tuck and Ty were on opposite sides of a girl in a Heru cheer uniform. They must have also pulled her to safety.

"What happened?"

"I don't know," Tuck answered. He carefully sat the cheerleader down next to Troy.

Sirens grew louder and the front of the school filled with first responders. Charcoal snow was falling. Troy had never been this close to a fire before. He never wanted to be this close to a fire again.

"This place isn't safe," the cheerleader scowled. Troy looked at her. Tuck and Ty looked at her too.

"What are the chances that a fire breaks out during one of the biggest school rivalry football games?" Troy turned around to see a guy in a black sweater. He looked around the courtyard. There had to be at least forty people there. Mostly in black and gray, but a few wearing red, blue and yellow.

"This was probably done on purpose," Ty said.

"By who?" The guy in the blue letterman spoke up. "Sure as hell wasn't us." Troy saw that it was the same guy who helped Ty pull him to safety.

"Why would we burn up our own school," Tuck was getting angry.

"Is everyone ok over here?" They all turned around. Approaching paramedics interrupted the would-be fight.

The cheerleader was seen first, then the guy in the black sweater. Tuck and Ty helped Troy to the nearest ambulance, while they discussed the strange event.

The police came by while a paramedic observed Troy's leg. "Did any of you guys see what happened?" A cop walked up holding a tablet.

Troy shook his head.

"Man, tell her what you told us," Ty urged.

"I didn't really see anything," Troy snarled.

"Anything can help, young man. It's a lot of people out here hurt today. That fire might not have been an accident."

It took twenty minutes for the school to calm. Twenty minutes for people to stop running and the fire department to extinguish the fire. It looked like Troy would walk away with a few bruises, but not everyone was that lucky. At least three ambulances left with their sirens sounding.

"Are you a Panther or a Falcon?" Troy asked. The cop looked up from the tablet. Troy couldn't decide if she was confused or didn't hear the question. "If you came to this game today, but you weren't working, what color would you have worn?"

The cop sighed and dropped her hands to her side. Tuck and Ty looked at her. They were waiting on her answer too.

"Would you have worn blue or black?" Ty asked.

"What does it matter?" The cop asked.

"It matters," Troy huffed. "I ain't see nothing."

"What color do I need to have on for you to have seen something?" She asked. She looked at the boys. Troy and Ty both wore black and gray lettermans over black and gray T-shirts, his adorned with a chess patch while Ty's was decorated with all of his sports and activities. Tuck just wore a black hoodie. "I'm a panther," she finally answered.

Troy didn't necessarily believe her, but she gave him the right answer. He told her how he saw two guys disappear into the parking lot wearing what looked like panther T-shirts, but they clearly weren't panther T-shirts. The cop almost laughed until she realized they were serious.

"They had on gray shirts?" The paramedic interjected. Troy slowly nodded his head. "Something is definitely fishy about that."

The cop looked at them all slowly before typing on her tablet. "Did you get a good look at these guys?"

Troy could tell she thought this was stupid. "They looked like every other student. One had a fade, one wore a baseball cap. Another had on basketball shorts in 50 degree weather."

"Any tattoos or identifying marks. Maybe, I don't know… piercings."

Troy's face scowled. Cops were always talking to you like you were dumb. "Why would I notice something like that?"

"Thank you gentlemen," the cop left.

Troy didn't really think their rival school would burn their school down. Of course they embarrassed them on the football field during halftime, but that shouldn't make them want to burn down their school?

"You may be on to something," Ty said. "Those falcons are really aggressive. You see those guys tried to fight us because they were embarrassed about the halftime show. All of their students are probably like that."

"Over a stupid rivalry," Tuck interjected. "Come on now. You athletes really do take this thing too far."

"They tried to rush us man."

"Friendly competition man. Just friendly competition," Tuck smiled.

Troy was so stunned about the fire that he forgot what happened before that. While he and Ty were waiting for Tuck to catch up, two guys in falcon letterman's pushed up against Ty. He was so lost in his thought that he didn't even pay attention. Everything had happened so fast.

Every Falcon vs Panther game was a city-wide event. It was friendly competition most of the time, but sometimes things would get out of control. Mostly between the football and basketball teams, but sometimes the band, the baseball team and even the chess team may have a disagreement. It was usually just words about how the other team sucked, nothing too major. A few jokes here and there, but not a school fire. How did that happen so fast?

The paramedic asked Troy if he wanted to go to the hospital. It could be a torn ligament or a sprain, but his injuries didn't seem severe. He'd only take him if he wanted to go.

"Nah, I'm good. Thanks man," Troy responded as Ty and Tuck helped him out of the ambulance. A few others quickly took their place.

Ty ran to fetch his car while Tuck waited with Troy. "You think we having school Monday?" Tuck asked him.

Troy glanced at the charcoal that lined his school. He shrugged.

"You up for the after party?" Ty asked as he helped Troy into the passenger seat. Troy drew a blank expression as he thought about it. "I can always drop you at home," Ty smiled.

"How else am I going to find out what happened?" Troy responded.

"That's my boy." Tuck slid in the back while Ty ran back to the driver's seat.

Troy could tell when they pulled up to the house that the party wasn't going to be the same. "Where everybody at?" Tuck questioned.

"We left before the game ended," Troy responded. "No one wanted to witness the rest of that embarrassment.

"Pretty sure that game is over. Even if it wasn't over," Tuck said.

Troy watched as a few people trickled into Ginelle's two story, brick house.

"Ginelle's not going to like this," Ty observed. "Especially because of how fire Sherray's party was last night."

"Fire," Troy said, "I see what you did there."

"Does everything really have to be a competition?" Tuck asked.

"Yup." Ty opened Troy's door. "You really need to get some crutches man. I'm not trying to carry yo ass around." Tuck helped Ty assist Troy into the house.

"Oh my god," Ginelle screamed when she saw Troy being carried. She acted like he was the walking dead. "Did this happen in the fire?"

"Yea, my boy was single handedly rescuing people when half the building fell down on him," Ty started, "It's amazing he's alive." The boys looked at each other and laughed.

"Shouldn't he be at the hospital," Ginelle asked.

"That's no place for heroes," Tuck explained.

"I'll just find a seat inside," Troy said. He didn't need the guys offering anymore lies on his behalf, although he was grateful that they had. No one needed to know the real story. Hopefully no one saw him cowering on the ground like a baby.

Troy sat on the couch and pretended to be fine as people filed in one by one with their own versions of what had happened. The party wasn't a party at all. It was a rumor mill. No one's story sounded the same, but it didn't take long before the blame game caught steam. Only a few Heru students showed up and it seemed they only did so to start the fight.

The only thing people seemed to agree on was that the Heru falcon's must have been responsible and the Panther's had no choice but to get revenge.

3 KELVIN MCGARRH

Kelvin didn't understand why he was in the hospital. He felt fine. He couldn't wait for his mom to get there so he could be discharged.

"Here you go sweetie, but you need to take it easy." The nurse gave him a plastic bag. What he wanted most was staring right at him. He ripped open the bag to grab his phone. The screen was black. He held down the power button. "You were really lucky."

She had already told him that. She was the first person he saw when he woke up. She told him his arms were wrapped in gauze to protect his burns. She told him that most of his burns were second degree, but they would heal nicely. She told him that his mom had called and she was on her way. What she didn't tell him was what he wanted to know. She couldn't tell him what happened at the school. Of all the kids she claimed were hurt, she didn't know any of their names or what school they went to. She didn't know anything of importance except where his phone was.

54 missed messages and he was going to read them all. He looked up and she was still staring at him. She was still talking, but he didn't know why. "Can I have some water?" he asked.

She looked offended that he interrupted her, but she fell silent. She poured a cup of water from the table that was right next to him. He didn't know how he had missed that.

His phone chirped. They both looked at it. "Well, can I get something to eat?"

"Sure honey," she sighed. She gave him the water and finally she understood what he wanted. She left the room.

54 messages from three people. His mom, his dad and his best friend. They all wanted to know the same thing. Where he was. *I have got to get some more friends,* he thought. *I have to find a sport. I bet the chess team even gets more messages than this.*

Kelvin responded to his best friend since he knew his mom and dad had already figured out where he was. "Ouch!" he exclaimed. His right hand hurt. Maybe that's why it was mostly wrapped in gauze. He decided to type with just his left hand even though it took twice as long.

He stalked social media for answers. There were plenty pictures of people running and crying. A few people started using #epicschoolprank as a hashtag, but it seemed like no one really knew what had happened. That fire was dangerous. Could it have really been a prank?

The sun was out. They should know who burned up the Panther's school by now. He remembered seeing the loyal blue, bold gold and righteous red, adorn the panthers poor school before it erupted in flames. It wasn't there long, but it was definitely there. Could the Heru Falcon's really be responsible? Why was that the last thing Kelvin saw before those flames burned through his flesh?

He sat his phone on his lap and sipped the water as he thought. He was trying to leave the game early. He was looking for his best friend so they could get to the after party. He couldn't wait to get to high school just because of the parties. He was going to stand out in a good way. This party was going to be the debut of his new kicks. Custom sneakers with the fight scene from his favorite anime adorned the sides.

They preferred the Panther's party to the Heru party because less people would know them. Both schools went to the pre party and the after party, but the hosting school always had more of their own students. Kelvin could blend in with anyone at the Panther party. They wouldn't know him so someone would have to think he was cool. This year, a panther student was hosting the after party. Maybe if Kelvin waited until the end of fourth quarter he wouldn't spend his Saturday morning in a hospital bed.

His ringing phone broke his thoughts. He dropped it as soon as he grabbed it. His right hand really hurt. Maybe he should have listened to that nurse. He picked it back up with his left hand. "Hello?" It was his best friend.

"The hospital? You really scared me man. At first I thought you went to the party without me, but when you never answered my texts or calls, I started thinking the worst."

"What do you mean the worst?" Kelvin hadn't had a chance to think about it, "Did someone die?"

"A lot of people were hurt, Kel. I don't know. It was really chaotic. What happened? Are you okay?"

Kelvin didn't know the answer to that question. He felt fine. At least he thought he felt fine. "I just remember..." he paused. He only remembered seeing their school colors foaming around their rival school. He talked through his thoughts. "You went to the bathroom right? I was going to wait for you at the car."

"Yea, that's the last time I saw you."

Kelvin remembered Heru had just scored another touchdown. No one was surprised, they seemed to always win the football game. A lot of people were leaving. The halftime shows were done. Everyone knew who would win. The only thing left was the after party.

"Did you make it to the party?" Kelvin asked, jealously awaiting the answer.

"I was there for a little while. Mostly looking for you. They said some kids got burned really bad. Some got trampled. It got really uncomfortable because the Panthers were starting to think it was someone from our school that did it. I almost got into a fight."

"You? A fight? How'd that happen?" Kelvin was attentive to Clover's growing popularity, but a fight would surely ruin that.

"I was minding my business, grabbing some of the snacks from the dessert table when I heard a few panthers getting all loud talking about that fire being a prank. Something that we caused."

"Yea, I saw a few people mention something like that on Insta."

"I laughed because I thought it was preposterous. Arson isn't a prank. It's a crime. But I didn't think anyone even heard me. I was really just kinda laughing to myself. Well some guy who limped into the party spotted me."

"Spotted you?" Kelvin questioned. "Who knows you?" Kelvin didn't mean for it to sound as bad as it did, but he knew his friend wouldn't take offense.

"From the chess team man. It was probably the same guy who did that paint prank."

Kelvin knew what he was referring to. Clover was on the chess team and at one tournament, of all the schools present, the panthers chess team pulled a prank on them. There was no proving it, but everyone knew it was them. The black bleachers the Heru chess team sat on were coated with fresh black paint. After looking around to find where the paint smell came from, one of his teammates realized that the back of his jacket and pants were black. Seconds later, they all realized they were painted black. Something only panthers would do.

"What did he say?" Kelvin asked.

"He said, of course a falcon would think that's funny. He was loud. Everyone started looking at me. One of his friends rushed over to me. I didn't even know what he was talking about until he pushed me, then said, you're probably the one that did it. Trying to get us back from that paint your team wore at the chess match."

"Aw man," Kelvin knew Clover wasn't a fighter, "what did you do?"

"I just backed away. Told him I didn't know what he was talking about. Another falcon was there because someone yelled about that halftime performance and the guy started arguing with them next. I was already trying to leave when a girl yelled for us all to get out. The cops were walking up the lawn as I left."

"Man... that's crazy." Burning down the school was one hell of a prank, but the schools were always trying to outdo themselves. "So, do you think it was some sort of prank?"

Clover sighed, "I have told you over and over again that I am not part of the society."

"That's not what I was hinting at," Kelvin chuckled. Although that was exactly what he was hinting at. "I just thought maybe you might have heard something."

"Channel 4 is rerunning that clip about their principal yelling at the superintendent. This is about to get ugly."

"I'm in the hospital, man. It's already ugly."

"I'm just happy you're okay. It was crazy. People were running everywhere. My trip to the bathroom may have saved me."

"What did you see after you came out the bathroom?"

"People going crazy. Security blocked off the gate. All I knew was that we couldn't leave the stadium. I thought it was a fight or a shooter until I saw the flames. We had to wait for them to get the fire out. Outside the gate it looked like everyone was running mad. The parking lot was full of ambulances. Every ambulance in the city must have been there. I don't know how many people were hurt. I'm sure you saw more than I did. What did you see on your way to the car?"

Kelvin hadn't given much thought to what happened at the game. He was too consumed with trying to get out of the hospital. He remembered leaving the stadium through the gate. He passed by a few fans from each side. A small altercation with a few athletes, then he made it to the front of the school. He slowed down when he heard a girl about twenty feet in front of him say, "What the hell is that?" He turned around. The same thing that caught her eye, caught his. Before he knew it, he was walking closer to the entrance. He remembered smiling at the sight of his school colors. He thought it was a celebratory thing. He thought the lights and sizzle were going to be fireworks, until fire was coming directly toward him.

He remembered the fireball landed on his head. In his smooth hair. His right arm is what he used to bat at the fire that was burning his skin. He moved his arm almost instinctively. First, his palm brushed against the top right side of his head, but it was too hot. He used his arm to rub until he finally fell to the ground trying to smother the flame with the grass.

His hair. His head…He jumped out of bed. Making sure to lean toward his left so as not to injure his right arm again. Was he one of those victims that his friend was talking about?

"Kel?! Kelvin?!" He could hear his best friend through the phone that still lie on the bed.

The bathroom? He knew there had to be a mirror in there. The door was open. Something tugged at his arm as he walked. He realized cords attached to his arm led to bags hanging from a pole. "An IV?" He snatched the pole and pulled it with him to the bathroom. His reflection scared him.

Part of his hair was missing. His eyebrow was gone. The brown skin above his right eye was no longer smooth and now had traces of white, red and pink. There was a draft behind him. He looked down and realized he was wearing a gown. He was naked underneath. Suddenly he was in pain.

4 JEREMY ROBINSON

Jeremy had a long night, but he couldn't ignore the text he had received that morning. He showed up in the gym of Huey P. Newton high school with the rest of the coaching staff. They all sat in the bleachers awaiting Corbin. Corbin called a mandatory meeting and Jeremy had a feeling that he knew what the meeting would be about.

He should have known sooner or later these rivalry school pranks would get out of hand. They never stayed innocent that long. There was that huge fight his basketball team had two and a half years before in their game against Heru. It was his first year coaching then. He had seen rivalry before. He had seen fights between teams before, but he had never seen anything like that.

His team was winning. Beating the Heru basketball team was something the Panthers had grown accustomed to, but this lead was embarrassing. One of his players was the cockiest player he had ever seen in his twenty year basketball career. Colby had shot three after three. Even a novice player should have seen it coming, but Heru did not have the skillful players that they have now. It wasn't enough that everything Colby did made both crowds go wild. One cheering him on, the other trying to distract him, but he couldn't be distracted.

Colby gloated after each point. Sometimes he'd roar, sometimes he'd run around like a flying bird, sometimes he'd do a little dance. The crowd ate it up. He was the one running the show. Normally, Jeremy wouldn't allow his players to do this type of antics, but he couldn't believe the response. Even Corbin ate it up. It was his first year in the district and as the head coach of one of the most promising teams he had come across, he didn't want to make a bad impression. Perhaps he also got wrapped up in Colby's show.

The last straw was when he ran over to kiss one of Heru's cheerleaders on her cheek. It happened so fast that the Panther's didn't notice until one of the players from Heru ran to Colby and punched him in his face. That was all that was needed for a riot to start. Before Jeremy knew it his entire team was in the middle of the court fighting Heru's entire team. It didn't take long before the cheerleaders joined, followed by the fans.

Jeremy had seen nothing like it, but that wasn't what stunned him the most. It seemed like more people were running to join the fight instead of trying to stop the fight. It took the police and the fire department to bring order back into the stadium. As if that wasn't enough, the news reports after the altercation were all over the place. One story said only two people were hurt. Another said that a fight broke up the game. Some accounts blamed Heru while some blamed the Panthers, but neither was right. Neither told of the knockdown, drag out, brawl that ensued the entire stadium. It was a riot and Jeremy was left thinking perhaps he had made the entire thing up.

"What was that?" He asked his assistant coach the next week. Once he was able to come to his senses.

"Sometimes the rivalry gets out of hand. Don't worry, it never seems to go that far."

"That was a riot. A war zone!" Jeremy had urged him.

"It was bad," his assistant coach agreed, "but it wasn't that bad. No one died."

Wasn't that bad? Jeremy thought about those words. What would his then assistant coach say if he saw this? The entire entrance of the school was gone.

"I'm sure you're all aware of why I called this meeting today." Corbin settled the coaching staff with his entrance. Jeremy looked around as the other coaches gave Corbin their attention and nodded in agreement. Corbin continued, "I spoke to the fire marshal this morning and they're almost certain this is a case of arson. It won't take long before we have more details."

No one was shocked to hear this information. The staff listened intently waiting for Corbin's next words. "I'm pretty sure our students would never do anything such as deface the pride and joy of our school, but some of them may have some answers. Some of you may have some answers. All of this nonsense seems to spur from our athletic departments. I thought I was clear about our teams focusing on points not revenge, but perhaps I wasn't clear enough. This is the type of thing that happens when this rivalry gets out of hand. After twenty years, you would think it wouldn't come to this."

Jeremy swallowed and looked around nervously. He hoped his boys didn't have anything to do with the rivalry, but he was pretty sure they did. How much did Corbin expect them to interfere with the students behavior? He couldn't be sure that his players were involved.

"Starting with that little halftime stunt. How did we end up with the falcon mascot?" Corbin stood right in front of the football coach, waiting for an answer.

"I don't know Corbin. I'm pretty sure the band had something to do with that. I'm just responsible for the players," he shrugged nervously.

"My kids just put on a performance," the band instructor didn't even wait for Corbin to look at him. He was in defensive mode. "Someone has to make the panther fans want to come to the game. They sure as hell don't show up for the football team." A few of the other coaches chuckled. The football team was the only sports program at Panther high that seemed to consistently fail against the Heru falcons.

Corbin walked closer to the band director. "Are you sure you don't know anything about stealing the Falcon's mascot?" He rested his hand on his chin. "That halftime show seemed flawless down to the choreography."

"I can show you our practice tapes," the band instructor defended. "We practiced with a picture of the Falcon's mascot. I don't know where that mascot came from."

"How did he know the routine? He has to be someone in the band?" the football coach accused.

"The band is huge. Over two hundred people knew that routine. Come on man." The band director sighed.

Corbin looked around as if he was considering what they were both saying. He looked around as if looking for a more appropriate suggestion. "So no one knows who was in the mascot uniform?"

"Even if we knew, how would that help us find out who burned our school?" The tennis coach spoke up. A few coaches nodded in agreement.

"Because I need answers!" Corbin barked. He sighed and shook his head. Jeremy had never heard him raise his voice. From the look on the other coaches' faces, they hadn't either. "I'm sorry," his voice was softer now. "We just need to get to the bottom of this. I could only imagine what your players would have done if that was our mascot that was stolen. That might have been enough to piss off the falcons. I don't know." Corbin studied each of the coaches' faces. "If you guys know anything. No matter how small, please tell me."

Jeremy wondered if he should say something. No one else looked like they would. But he did know something. The afternoon before the game, Jeremy was in his office doing some paperwork. Paperwork that he should have done on Thursday, but he was too lazy to do. He heard a few of his players in the back of the gym laughing. He went out to find out what was going on. They looked stunned to see him. He was actually stunned to see them. Colby said, "What's up coach," while Kedric stood quickly in front of the bag. The huge blue bag was hard to hide. It wasn't until the halftime show did he realize he saw yellow feathers outside of the bag. It was only for a second. He could have been mistaken.

"What y'all doing here?"

"We could ask you the same question." Colby joked. Jeremy didn't smile. He didn't play with his players. If his career taught him anything, he knew if you gave these players an inch they would take a foot. Colby dropped his smile, then cleared his throat. "I left my good shoes in the locker. We just stopped here so I could pick them up."

Jeremy knew that answer didn't make sense, but at least he had one. He went back to his office to finish his paperwork. That was it. That's all he thought he saw, but he didn't think he should say anything.

The staff said they wanted answers, but he knew better. No one would really talk. Corbin gathered all of the coaches because he knew it was the athletes that pulled off all rivalry pranks. It was an unspoken rule. Everyone knew it, but no one said it. The less you knew, the less you said. The rivalry had been brewing much longer than Jeremy knew and much longer than he wanted to know.

The more Jeremy thought about it, the more he knew he should keep his mouth shut. Everyone knew the players had a pre-game party and a post-game party around the football game. Apparently this was an ancient tradition that was forbidden two and a half years before. After that basketball stunt. He asked the cheer coach after he overheard her telling her squad to be careful.

"I thought they couldn't have those parties anymore," he knew better to ask her when no one was around.

"Yea, but they're just kids and I know my girls will be careful?"

"What if something else dangerous happens?"

"That's a big maybe. And besides, we knew nothing about it," she gave a sly smile.

"Are they sure it wasn't electrical?" The soccer coach broke his thoughts.

"I think the fire marshal is a falcon. I don't think we'll get a fair inspection. He's trying to blame everyone that's not a Falcon," Corbin responded.

That was the type of response Jeremy had grown accustomed to. To panthers, if something was wrong, the culprit had to be a falcon. To falcons, it was the other way around. Jeremy was still shocked at the accusations Corbin made against the superintendent. That type of behavior would have never happened in any other district.

"Not for long," the chess coach offered. "Have you seen that video circulating?"

"I just saw it before this meeting," the golf coach added, "it was definitely a falcon."

This was news to Jeremy. Apparently it was news to Corbin as he looked around the room in confusion. "What video?" He finally asked.

Corbin didn't finish his question before someone had a phone in his hand. Jeremy looked around the room as more of his colleagues turned to show each other their phones. Someone finally handed him a tablet with the video on the screen. The caption said, Epic School Prank. Jeremy could tell by the little symbol at the bottom of the video that it was being shared over and over again. It didn't take long for him to know why. The falcons had a lot of explaining to do.

5 KEIANNA BROWN

Keianna was becoming an overnight celebrity. She had never had this many views on her account. All because she was at the right place at the right time. This was better than being behind some stupid prank.

She should have known something was going to happen. The panthers stealing the falcon's mascot was grand, but it caused an eerie feeling in the air. She remembered being in the stands near the end of the halftime show, hearing the sound of what she thought was a wounded panther. It was like a roar gone wrong. None of her friends heard it. She looked around, but it seemed like no one else heard it either. People were going up or down the bleacher stairs, checking their phones and laughing at the halftime show, but nothing seemed out of place to them.

The players could barely finish out the game without disagreements starting on the field. She and her friends usually left the Heru vs Newton football game sometime during the third quarter, like most people did. Just long enough to make sure the Panther's wouldn't finally win against them. It was clear that they wouldn't. The referees ended up calling the game early. Right after she left the stadium gates.

She smiled as she watched her video on the local news. Right there in the corner it said, courtesy of prettygirlkei. She couldn't wait until school Monday. That is… if there was school Monday. She hoped they found a way to open the school. People would have so many questions for her and she'd bask in all the glow of admiration. This popularity would surely overshadow her past.

It amazed her how a single second made such a difference in her popularity. Her friend had stopped walking with her for a second to flirt with some guys from Heru. She of course would never do that again. She was minding her own business in front of the school. She'd post a few pictures to waste time. She used her phone as a mirror to fix her makeup. She pulled all of her hair over her right shoulder to make sure the soft curls were still there. She liked how the parking lot light made her hair glow. She snapped a picture. #nofilter.

Some guy in a green shirt with a soft voice stood right next to her. She didn't even see who he was but heard when he said, *what the hell is that?"* She immediately held her phone up to record.

The front of her school was covered in bright, fluffy colors. On the right it was red, the front was in yellow and only seconds later, the left was in blue. It was undeniably the color of the falcons. She was about to announce her disgust when the flames stole her surprise. She instinctively walked backwards because she felt the heat from the flames, but she kept her phone focused on the scene. Through the sounds of the fire, she could hear people yell and scream in amazement, but she kept her eyes glued on her money maker. She smiled because she was catching it all on video. She knew right then that her video was going to be worth something. She was going to sell to the highest bidder. She began collecting business cards from the first reporters that appeared at the school.

The entire video was 32 seconds and she analyzed every one of them. She wished it was longer. Yellow and red foam covered the school at the same time, with blue covering it only 2 seconds later. The yellow and red were already there when she managed to turn the camera direction and start recording, but the blue definitely came from the bottom and shot up to cover the school. The foam didn't start from the roof, like some people thought. It started from the ground.

Eight seconds after that, a fire grew from the red side and quickly swallowed all of the foam. The Panthers had perfectly manicured landscape around the front of the school. Evergreen bushes wrapped around the sides of the school and met in the front, right next to the panther shaped bushes that flanked the front steps. The panther shaped bushes weren't real, but they matched the real evergreen bushes right next to them. The twin panthers stood on their hind legs, nine feet tall. Piercing claws extended from their fore paws and their teeth looked sharp as thorns. It was a tourist attraction. Something that every panther was proud of. Visitors, students and alumni alike all had pictures in front of the perfect panthers. Panthers that disintegrated in eight seconds.

That part hurt, but Keianna knew that Mr. Dossani would rebuild. The new panthers would probably be twice or three times as large. Her newfound fame would replace the hurt. Besides, they still had Huey. The statue of Huey P. Newton was closer to the curb and it was untouched. But everyone knew not to touch the hero. To deface his statue would be a cardinal sin.

Keianna kept filming as long as she could. 15 seconds after the flames started, the running crowd was growing larger. People were bumping into her and she was scared she would get knocked over, or worse, drop her phone. The last seconds were of a guy in a Heru letterman, pulling on a pretty girl in yellow, red and blue calf length braids, wearing an ugly sweater. She seemed to be running toward the fire while he was pulling her to the parking lot. Keianna was almost certain both of them were Heru students. Her hair matched his shoes. Maybe a couple. When she realized who the guy was, she stopped recording.

The next time she began recording she was sitting on top of her car filming the fire trucks putting out the fire. She wiped the sweat that formed on her forehead from the heat of the flame. She hand-parted her hair so that she could pull each half over a shoulder. She refreshed her lipstick before centering herself in the frame, making

sure the camera could see her hair resting right above her lap. "I
don't know what's happening," she exclaimed. She held a
bewildered look for two seconds before turning her phone camera
towards the scene around her. That video was watched by many, but
not nearly as many as her first video. Everyone had a video of the
screaming students, the fire, the ambulance and the fire trucks. Only
she had the video of the foam turning into flames.

She watched injury after injury, limp, scream and run from the fire
until she couldn't take anymore. Keianna didn't understand the
severity of the situation until she saw a charred figure being rushed
to an ambulance truck. She stayed long enough to make sure all of
her friends were accounted for before rushing to the after party. The
school was nothing but chaos. If you were an able body, the police
forced you to leave the area. The after party was the only place to get
information or so Keianna thought.

When they pulled up at Ginelle's house the police were instructing
people to keep driving. Students were walking away from the house
instead of towards it. The party had been shut down. "How did they
get there so fast?" Keianna questioned as she drove slowly past the
house. She could tell the party was going to be epic because people
who had obviously been hurt could be seen leaving. She recognized
the tall one who joined with an unknown round guy to help the
wounded. His picture adorned the sports champion wall. If they
were helping their friend to the party instead of the hospital, it had to
be lit.

"Apparently," Amaris called from the back seat. "A huge fight broke out. People think the falcons burned down our school." She was looking at her phone.

"No way," Karissa snatched the phone away. "They wouldn't do that. Would they?"

"I don't know," Keianna said after finally passing Ginelle's house. "Their colors were all over the school immediately before the fire started."

"What you mean by that?"

Keianna explained to her friends everything she saw. They kept circling the block hoping to find somewhere else to go. After they accused her of lying the fourth time, she pulled over and showed them the video.

"You gotta post this."

"I want to see if the news will pay me for it first."

"Girl, please. All those people that were out there. What if they already posted it first?"

Keianna didn't care what her friends said. She was going to wait it out and she almost made it to the next morning, but no one would budge. The news didn't even entertain her until after she posted it on her page, but by then, they had public access. At least her name was associated with it. They had to at least give her credit. And just in case they didn't. Her brother made her put a watermark on it before she posted it anyway. And it turned out that no one else had footage.

She was in the right place at the right time.

She originally stalled hoping for real currency, but soon realized she'd have to settle for social currency. She was cool with that. Sometimes clout was more important than money. And she needed to be known by more than a Panther who dated Falcons.

She was up all night reading posts, calling friends and hearing rumors about what had happened. People in other districts were calling it an epic school prank. It made sense to her. She had seen plenty of rival pranks over the years. It was one of the things that made her so excited to go to high school. She was closest to Huey P. Newton, so it wasn't a question of if she would be a panther. She had been wearing black and gray since elementary. Usually the schools made fun of each other, but nothing ever this horrible. Outside of a fight here and there, the pranks were usually innocent. Who would have thought they would burn down their school? What was Pantherland going to be like without the panthers protecting the entrance? What was the school going to be like without an entrance?

Keianna tried to drive by the school twice that morning, but the police wasn't letting anyone get near the school. You couldn't even drive down the street, but she could tell from the corner that the school entrance was not the same. All she could see was the concrete steps.

Game day was so weird. The sound. The people leaving right after she had. Her friend actually giving a Heru falcon the time of day after what she'd been through and of course the peak. She wished she could go back. Maybe pay attention more. She looked through the rest of the pictures on her phone. Before the fire, it was mostly pictures of her and her friends taking selfies. They wore black and gray and there was nothing, but black and gray in the background. Except for one picture. Keianna realized someone had on gray and black. The parking lot light made the waves in his head shine as they dispersed into a smooth tapered fade. Keianna laughed, he must have been new to the area.

6 CHEY HENRY

Chey thought that those Huey P. Panthers were really a piece of work. First they stole their mascot then blamed them for burning down their raggedy ass school. Chey was pissed. He created the most epic school prank and it was overshadowed by the halftime performance and that damn fire.

"Are y'all sure that y'all did everything exactly the way I asked you?" Chey stroked the hairs growing along his chin, while waiting for an answer. He held a private meeting at his home when he knew his parents would be away. He was always paranoid when it came to orchestrating the school pranks.

"C'mon bro. We know better." Augusta said. Augusta, D'Anthony, Calvin, Montreal and TJ were the masterminds for the most epic prank in history. Well, Chey actually considered himself the mastermind. They were simply accomplices.

"We know how flammable that stuff is, man," D'Anthony added.

"You also know that you were supposed to start when the alarm went off and you were late," Chey barked.

"My bad man…" D'Anthony apologized. "It was only for a second though."

"And what happened to your face?" The question was rhetorical. They all knew D'Anthony got into a scuffle at the after party even though Chey told them not to go. Chey knew D'Anthony would mess up. He always did something wrong. If he wasn't so worried about getting caught, he would have found a new team. They didn't have to do anything but follow directions. Chey secured prank money from Mr. JJ, got the steel drums to the school and hid them behind the bushes on all three sides. He measured and separated all the ingredients. He made sure to wear a neutral color, green, so that he wouldn't stand out. He even found a random girl to record by pointing out the prank to her.

"Did y'all make sure no one was smoking before you did it?" Chey asked.

"I had the riskiest, busiest side. But no… everything was perfect," Calvin said.

"Man it wasn't us. All we did was put foam in our school colors on their school. That's it. Besides, all of you guys made it to the car before those flames even started," Montreal said. Chey trusted Montreal even less than D'Anthony. That's why his only job was to be a lookout and to drive.

D'Anthony wanted a job so bad. Chey let him get the shirts and they were the wrong color. The second dumb thing he did was decide the sound of their alarm. As if a simple alarm clock notification wouldn't do. Chey knew he should have just asked the new guy from the chess team to join them, but he figured this was too large of a prank.

"Then what happened?" Chey was worried. He was very meticulous about school pranks. His pranks made an impact but were safe. No one had gotten hurt in any of his pranks before. Being charged with completing school pranks at Heru was like a secret society. As a matter of fact, most people called it a society, but the people involved knew it had no official name. They simply repeated one mantra that all society members knew. You had to be chosen and only the trusted were chosen. It was better than being on a sports team. He didn't know what idiot recruited D'Anthony.

Chey was chosen as a freshman by a junior. She was a star track athlete and a resident party host. She liked that he was smart and had no interest in becoming well-known. The prank committee wasn't official and there were no records. Someone recruited you, you proved that you were capable and then you recruited others. There was no telling how many people were in on a prank. If you weren't a part of any particular prank, you didn't know who was. Chey inherited D'Anthony. He would have never chosen him.

The first prank Chey participated in as a freshman was putting *I Wish I were a Falcon* bumper stickers on the back of all the panther cars that came to their basketball game. It was a subtle prank that had a huge impact. Security sat in the parking lot of basketball games for two years after that, but Heru was too sophisticated to repeat an old prank.

The next prank Chey participated in wasn't until the end of his sophomore year. Someone spray painted the middle of the Panther student parking lot to state *Loser's parking.* They even lined staked signs on the entrance of the parking lot that read the same. They did this all under moonlight. Chey's job was to scour the area for surveillance, disable surveillance equipment if he found any, which he didn't, and be a lookout until the graffiti artist was finished. He almost didn't see the great work they did, but one of the Panther students took a picture and posted it. That's when he realized that all his future pranks would need to be documented in a way that didn't lead back to him.

"Maybe they burned up their own school." TJ said.

"But why would they do that?" Montreal asked.

The pranks had died down. The panther's principal Mr. Dossani made a public statement that his school was not going to participate in any more pranks. If they did unbeknownst to him and he found out, they would be punished. They were going to follow what was right and not what was popular, like their namesake, Fred Hampton. This was right before Chey had finally decided to lead his first prank. Heru's principal agreed to Mr. Dossani's announcement, but he knew nothing about the secret society and no one in the society that Chey knew of would ever talk. If they did, it would only be to a legacy man. And legacy men wouldn't utter a word. That was just outside of the way they operated. He set up his junior prank as planned and he only needed two people to pull it off.

Chey had a veteran and a newbie help him. Chey was a future chemist. And he used chemical compounds whenever he could. Before the Heru vs Panther football game they snuck onto the field. All he needed was gasoline and a huge stencil to pull it off. His participants followed his lead but had no clue what they were doing until the game had started. In the middle of the field right around the Panther logo the words read, *I Wish I Were a Falcon.* The gas burned through the turf. The panthers had obviously tried to cover it with green paint, but it only made the matter worse. Mr. Dossani made a point to get on the loudspeaker to tell the crowd, "When they go low, we go high." The Heru principal agreed, the Panther's bleachers cheered and the Heru bleachers laughed. The Panthers thought they were all high and mighty because their namesake was a revolutionary and their mascot was named after one of the highest grossing movies of all time. Well Heru was named after an original deity. The first Christ to which all other religions would follow. Even the word hero is modeled after him. From that alone, the Falcons deserved respect.

"It was probably an insurance job," Augusta said. "You know how many homes went up in flames before the gentrifiers moved to the area. Quiet as it's kept, fire is a cheap method of demolition."

Chey looked at him. "A fire, right where we put highly flammable foam. Listen to yourself man. Did any of you tell someone about this? Someone who would want this so-called cheap method of demolition?" He studied each person's face looking for even a hint of guilt. Chey had to yell to show that he was serious. He hated having a soft voice. If it wasn't for the society, no one would take him seriously.

"Nah man… to go against the society," D'Anthony started.

"Would be to go against self," the rest of the guys finished the society's mantra.

"But Augusta has a point. Dossani be talking all holy, but remember how he's been acting since Mr. Smith got in office."

"You're right," Calvin said. "Wasn't he mad at Mr. Smith because he claimed he wouldn't fix something at their school?"

"And the panthers have been itching to do something since that prank last spring," TJ said.

The prank last spring was also one of Chey's pranks. He didn't include any of these guys so he knew not to say anything in particular about it. He knew Heru would lose the basketball game to the panthers, they always lose that basketball game, but he decided to make it fun. He was sure that's why fans showed up in the first place; to see if any pranks would happen.

He knew that the district had gotten fancy new digital scoreboards that year. So fancy, that it was easy for any computer whiz to hack it. And he had known the perfect unknown hacker since middle school to help. All game, Chey would trip the scoreboard to change who was the home team. By the time the officials realized what was happening, they lost count. After halftime, they decided the scores would have to be taken manually. The game wasn't as exciting because it was hard for the audience to really know what the score was. The Panther's still won, although not by as many points as they would have had the score been accurate. To make matters worse, their victory bell was overshadowed by a 90ft banner that fell after the game buzzard. The banner read, *I Wish I Were a Falcon*. The whole fiasco overshadowed the Panther's winning game. This was two weeks before Mr. Dossani's outburst at the school district's board meeting. He had grown furious with Heru's antics.

He demanded that the Superintendent get to the bottom of it. It took months for them to track down where the banner was sold, but Chey was always careful to cover his tracks. He had a random lady pick it up and pay cash for it in another city. There's no way that lady would know they were looking for her, she lived on the street. And even if they found her, she couldn't identify Chey if she wanted to. Other than finding a hacker who showed him how to strip the scoreboard, he acted alone in that prank. He never mentioned what he needed the hack for. He knew it couldn't get back to him, but he was still shook that they had even tried.

"That's why I'm happy we got our prank in because that mascot prank was pretty good," TJ said.

Chey wanted to object, but he was right. He knew he did his school proud. They'd be the laughingstock of the city if it wasn't for that foam, but their names had to be cleared. The focus had to be taken off of Heru.

"Why do you think the principal had something to do with it?" Chey inquired.

7 RENAE GRAY-BURLESON

It was not looking good at all. Renae was happy she was too busy with her girls to witness their school ablaze. The way all of her colleagues talked about it, it sounded like a nightmare. She knew one day those school pranks would go too far. Someone really needed to stop them from happening, but who?

Renae didn't understand why Mr. Dossani was adamant about school starting as normal. He knew the kids wouldn't be focused. The teachers couldn't even focus. Renae was sure that he wasn't focused either. He called a mandatory meeting during the top of first period. It would be just like Mr. Dossani to call school just so he could have a mandatory meeting.

Renae saw Mr. Dossani standing in the middle of the stage as soon as she entered the auditorium with her class. His deep brown eyes scanned every inch of the auditorium. Standing alone in the center of the stage made him seem like a giant. Unlike his true 5' 10" frame. He stood there until it appeared that no other classes would enter.

As soon as everyone was seated and fell silent, Mr. Dossani began to speak. "I know you're wondering why I called this meeting. Why school is still in session after something so disgusting happened to our glorious building. I just wanted to remind you that we are family and just like family, during times of turmoil, we must bind together and not fall apart." Someone started a slow clap until the entire auditorium joined.

Mr. Dossani continued to tell the audience that ten students were injured, eight from the Huey P. Newton and two from Heru. He named the eight students and asked the audience to send their prayers and if they wanted, they could donate to help the families. He visited each student over the weekend. All, but one was able to talk. He was in critical condition.

Renae gasped when she heard this information. She knew a lot of kids were hurt, but most that she knew of had minor cuts, burns and bruises. Nothing life threatening. Arson was bad enough, but this could potentially be murder.

"Not only the safety of our school, but the safety of our students has been compromised. I announced the end of school pranks years ago because I knew that this type of thing could happen and now, I hope that you all understand the severity of this.

"I know our athletes want more than anything, vengeance for these heinous acts, but it is you that I charge to be the example. That halftime prank seemed funny but look at the type of thing that could happen. I want to get to the bottom of this. I have to get to the bottom of this. All of your safety is in my hands. I want to start with identifying who was in the Heru Falcon mascot uniform."

The entire crowd grew restless. Renae knew the students hated every time Mr. Dossani mentioned stopping the rivalry. "I know what you're thinking," Mr. Dossani continued. "But this person may have information about the person responsible for this fire," he pleaded.

"Booooo," someone yelled from the back of the auditorium. Renae turned to the direction of the noise and heard another follow behind her. The students were taking turns disrupting their principal, but they were being careful not to get caught. The kids were good.

"Settle down students, settle down," Mr. Dossani commanded. After a few moments, the auditorium fell silent. Mr. Dossani continued, "You have my word that this person will not be in trouble at all. You all are my witnesses. Not even a letter will be added to their file. We simply must get to the bottom of this." He let his arms fall by his side and he looked at the audience. His piercing eye fell upon student and teacher alike. The audience was so quiet, you could've heard a pin drop.

Mr. Dossani finally stopped the silent treatment. "There's anonymous boxes around the school if you perhaps hear or know something and you're afraid to step forward. I am expecting to receive a letter from the district today. A copy will be emailed to all students, parents and teachers. The letter will also be on the homepage of every school's website and sent via phone message and text. I'm not sure what is said in the letter, but I can guess. The district wants to make sure we're all on the same page with ending these heinous pranks.

"Please keep our students in your prayers. Take time away from school if needed. Each student is granted at least five excused absences. You just have to reach out to our counseling program first."

"Will we rebuild?" A student yelled from the front of the auditorium.

"What about our panthers?" Another student yelled from the left of the auditorium.

Mr. Dossani looked in the direction of each question before bringing the mic back to his mouth. "Definitely."

Power to the People, Power to the Panthers, Power to the People, Power to the Panthers. The auditorium chanted with their fists raised until Mr. Dossani smiled and joined in the chant. Even Renae found herself inspired, yelling along with the auditorium.

Mr. Dossani excused the auditorium to return to class. Renae knew that she wasn't giving any lessons that day. She told her class to read from their textbooks, although she knew they'd spend more time talking. She pushed her glasses up the bridge of her nose. She twirled sprigs of hair from her afro as she pretended to look at her lesson plan.

"Does he really think we're going to turn in the mascot?" Her student, Colby, asked his classmates. Being a basketball player, Renae was pretty sure he knew all about the mascot fiasco, but she knew better than to ask. "For all we know it doesn't go against your academic career but starts your criminal career."

"Mr. Dossani has gone soft, man. He's still talking about *can we all just get along* even after these fools burn down our school? What happened to that energy from the school board meeting?" Kedrick said. Renae winced when she heard that.

"And we ain't no snitches," Colby purported before typing frantically on his phone. It wasn't long before Renae realized that all of the students were typing on their phone. She knew they were probably texting their classmates. She didn't care. She wasn't a big fan of Mr. Dossani anyway.

She never wanted to work at Huey P, but there were no vacancies at her alma mater, Heru High. She took the job, proving to her husband that she wasn't caught up in some silly rivalry, but she didn't think everyone else felt the same way.

"I guess not everyone wishes they were a Falcon," Mr. Dossani teased her in her interview. They both laughed and decided that the rivalry was old and stupid. It was something the students used to direct their energy towards since they didn't have real responsibilities.

It was the first of many regular teasings that she would receive. But she had grown to love the school, especially her job as cheer coach. She was upset when her older brother found out. He was a successful attorney who had moved away from the city, but still found a way to make their small school rivalry a big deal.

He scoffed when he saw her over the holidays wearing a black and gray T-shirt. "What in the world are you wearing?" Everyone within earshot turned to look at Renae.

They were in her house. She had opened the home she shared with her husband and kids to her siblings, their families and her parents for the holiday. She had countless gray and black T-shirts, hoodies, hats and jackets. Half of them were free. The panthers made sure there wasn't a shortage of school insignia.

As soon as Renae looked down at her shirt, she knew exactly what he was referring to. He was a running back when they were in school and she was a cheerleader. She couldn't believe that he still had such strong feelings about stuff that happened in high school.

"Greg, you didn't know that your sister is a Panther now?" her mom asked.

"Why did y'all let her do that?"

"Why not?" her dad added.

"Wow Greg," her husband spoke up. "Are you really on that rivalry thing too? Your parents mentioned you'd hate it, but I thought it was a joke."

"That was no joke. Because of them I missed my chance at a scholarship."

"Really, Greg!" Renae shrieked.

"Honey, you don't still believe that do you?" her mom asked.

"You're not the one who paid for school. I am," her dad made sure to remind him.

"I wanted to play football."

"But you ended up better than a football player. You're a big shot lawyer now. So in addition to thanking me for paying for school, you should also thank the panthers for interfering with your chances of getting that scholarship, so that you could focus on your studies in government." Her dad added.

"I could have went to the NFL!"

"Greg, you were not that good," Renae laughed. "You may have. May have," she stressed again, "been a college second string running back. Did you forget how many injuries you had?"

They made it through dinner without talking about the rivalry once Renae agreed to change her shirt. The entire topic may have been good as over if it wasn't for her dad bringing up the secret video she had.

"Renae, why don't you show Greg your principal at that meeting. He looks so familiar, but I cannot remember who he is to save my life," her dad recalled.

Renae felt the blood rush to her cheeks. Why did her dad mention that? She knew exactly who he was, she just told her dad that she didn't. She didn't tell anyone that she remembered because she didn't want to fester up old wounds.

"I deleted that video dad," she lied. It was funny then and she didn't even know why. It was before she felt vested in the school. Maybe because it was before she felt black and gray blood running through her veins. She showed her dad the stupid school board meeting video that she wasn't supposed to have been recording anyway. It was a closed meeting. She was new to the whole teaching thing and was trying to engulf herself into administration to see if that was a path she wanted to take.

"You're lying Renae. I can see it all over your face." Greg teased. "Now I really want to see it."

Renae knew that she couldn't lie to her brother. They were only a year apart. They grew up together. They were basically joined at the hip until he up and moved across the country. It didn't take long before she caved.

He watched as Mr. Dossani interrupted Grant while he talked of district progress. "You're lying. You can't believe this man. He's been lying since he was in high school. How dare you let him come back here and tell more lies."

"Please calm down," Grant said to Mr. Dossani. "I assure you, this was a board issue, not a me issue."

"That's Corbin, dad." Renae knew Greg would spot him in a second. "And Grant is the Superintendent? Where have I been?"

"Ahh," her dad wagged his finger. "I knew he looked familiar. All of your friends from your game days are back."

"My kids were promised part of that bond money. Our school was next for those improvements. How did we suddenly run out of money as soon as you took this position?" Mr. Dossani could be heard yelling through her phone.

Renae left the living room to get away from her dad and brother's accusations. They were starting to relive their high school days. Days that she was happy with being behind her. Somehow, them talking about it was making her feel like a traitor.

She was elated when she finally returned to the living room and saw her phone lying comfortably on the table. Her family was now yelling at the game on the TV. That was the end of it or so she thought, until she was called into her principal's office that next week.

"How was your break?" Mr. Dossani asked her as she sat across from his desk.

"It was good. I hadn't seen my brother in years and I finally saw him this year." She knew this wasn't a casual conversation. She hardly ever talked to her boss outside of cordial greetings or group settings.

"Yes, I know," Mr. Dossani calmly stated as he sat back in his chair.

Renae didn't know how he knew or why he'd care, but there she was, sitting across from him, hoping he couldn't hear the speed of her heartbeat through their silence.

"Oh, That's good," she finally spoke. She didn't know what to say. She realized that sounded like a dumb response, but she couldn't think of a more appropriate one. Mr. Dossani had to be the same age as her, but everything about him screamed authority figure. His eyes pierced her thoughts. She would confess everything she did if only she knew what she had done. She now knew why students didn't like to be called to the principal's office. If they felt like this every time they were called in, she was sure they'd prefer to just be suspended.

"Did you know that recording is not allowed in district meetings?"

That was it. She now knew why she had been called. Before he said another word she realized that her brother must have shown that video to someone who showed it to her boss. He saw her there that day. He knew that she was in the meeting. Maybe if she just took her husband's last name instead of that dumb hyphen, it wouldn't have even gotten back to him. Was she going to be fired?

"One of the board members called to remind me of my inappropriate behavior. I thought I had finally lived it down, but thanks to you and your brother, that will never happen."

She soon learned that her brother was careless with the video. He circulated it around his old high school buddies and it ended up on social media with the caption, *Some rivalries never die.*

Renae didn't want to take any responsibility, but she knew that was the fuel needed for the students to resuscitate the dying rivalry. As far as she knew, no one else knew that her brother and the current superintendent played high school football together at Heru High. That Mr. Dossani was the quarterback for the Huey P. Panthers at that time. That those guys are the reason this stupid high school rivalry started in the first place.

8 GINELLE REED

"So what are we going to do? We can't just sit around like Dossani is asking us to. We tried that already," Ty boasted. Ginelle could tell that he was angry.

"What do you suggest?" she asked. They sat in the corner of the cafeteria. They were mostly done eating lunch. She didn't have to hear the next table or the one next to that. Everyone was talking about the same thing. How to get revenge on the falcons.

"How they acted at your party. They probably came just to see our sad faces. To rub it in. They're lucky the police showed up, man."

"We don't even know if it was them. You heard what some people are saying?" Darryl lowered his voice. "They think Mr. Dossani had something to do with it."

"Man that's the dumbest shit I have ever heard." Ty barked.

"Didn't you see that video that leaked of him yelling at Mr. Smith? It could be true. This may be the real prank. He burns his own school and then blames it on Mr. Smith. Think about it, that's pretty epic?"

"You think he'd put all these kids in danger?" Ginelle questioned. She had seen some interesting pranks, but this one sounded risky to her.

"Maybe he didn't intend for anyone to get hurt. Remember the game ended early. Maybe he just didn't know the game would end early. That it would be so many kids out there."

"Mmm... I don't know. People always leave that game early. Still sounds weak to me."

"So you want to be a falcon now, Darryl. That sounds like something they would say. Did your cousin put you up to this? Are you really undercover?" Darryl looked offended. No one wanted to be called a falcon. Not right now. Right now there were only two sides and no matter if you chose one or not, you were definitely on one. Ginelle and Ty knew that Darryl had a cousin who attended Heru.

"You're either with us or against us," Ty said.

"Alright man," Darryl said. "You know my blood is black and gray. It's just one hell of a coincidence."

Ginelle could at least agree with that. It was one heck of a coincidence. It wasn't just Mr. Dossani's anger, it was his last words:

My kids will get their school improvements by any means necessary. That was a strange choice of words. The damage was done to the worst part of the school. They needed new paint at the entrance, but that couldn't be done without new wood. Apparently there were foundation issues, so it made no sense to add on top of that. The school district kept patching up the problems, but they would never completely fix them.

Everyone knew that Mr. Dossani pled with the district for renovations every year. He talked about it at every sports game, in every letter to staff, students and parents. He somehow found a way to bring it up in every school assembly.

"I wouldn't be surprised if the falcons knew how bad Mr. Dossani wanted those enhancements," Ginelle added. "What if they're trying to frame him? You know Mr. Dossani is always wanting us to stop these stupid pranks, maybe they're using that against him."

"See!" Ty exclaimed. He jumped out of his seat. "That's what I'm talking about. They come up with the craziest pranks. Stuff no one would ever think of. I wouldn't be surprised if they found Dossani guilty, let him spend ten years in prison and then fly a damn helicopter sign across our school that reads," he put his hands above his head then spread them apart as he stated, "You Wish you Were a Falcon".

Ginelle and Darryl started laughing at the same time. "You tripping, bae." Ginelle grabbed his arm and directed him to return to his seat.

"Whatever is going on, I'm telling you, this has Heru written all over it. They are so sneaky."

"You might be giving them too much credit," Darryl said. "If they're that good, how did we get their mascot?"

Ty pointed his finger aggressively at Darryl. "See," then he tapped that same finger on the table a few times. "That's what I'm talking about." He jumped out of his seat again. He walked away quickly before walking right back to the table. He slammed both of his hands onto the table and sighed. "How do we know they didn't let us steal their mascot just so they could do that?" He stood back up straight and put his hands on his hip, then he gestured at Darryl. "Just so you could say something like that. They slick, man." He shook his head.

Ginelle and Darryl were both fighting back laughter. "It'll be over soon. The fire marshal will figure out what happened and we'll be back to our stupid innocent rivalries. I need a do over anyway. The police crashed my party. It was going to be the best after party yet," Ginelle said.

"That's what I'm saying," Ty said in a loud whisper. He walked away then walked back quickly. "The fire marshal is a Heru alumni," he squealed. "Do you really think he'll find them guilty of anything?"

"What y'all talking about?" Joey sat down at their table, next to Darryl.

"All of these damn coincidences," Darryl said.

"What do you think?" Ginelle rolled her eyes.

"Ha! Heru trying to burn down our school?" Joey asked as he took a bite of his sandwich. "They wrote snitches get stitches and stop snitching on all the boxes Mr. Dossani put around the school.

"What you think, Joey?" Ty asked. "You think Heru burned down our school or Dossani?"

"Heru, no doubt," he muffled in between bites. He took a swig from his soda before adding, "my boy in the hospital fighting for his life behind this bullshit."

"See," Ty stopped speaking abruptly.

Pictures of the burned student started circulating the school. Most people still didn't know who he was, but Renae knew he looked familiar. She suddenly realized that she had seen him with Joey several times. She closed her gaped mouth. "How is he?" She asked slowly.

Joey took another bite of his sandwich and shook his head. "I don't even know," he dropped his sandwich on his tray. "He didn't deserve this."

"Is there anything we can do?" Ginelle asked. Her face now long.

Ty finally took his seat next to her. He watched as Joey took a sip of his soda before shaking his head. "That's why they gotta pay." Ginelle elbowed him in his arm. "Ouch," Ty shrieked.

She didn't know what got into Ty. He was really into this revenge. Revenge that she didn't even know if it was necessary. As long as she could remember, there was a rivalry between the falcons and the panthers, but it never got out of control. There had to be a reasonable explanation. She had heard that the fire marshal said arson, but maybe he made a mistake. How do they determine that anyway?

"How was your party?" Darryl looked at Ginelle. She knew that he knew the answer. He was trying to change the subject.

"It was..." she thought for a second. "Short."

"They shut it down," Ty said. "The party hardly got started before those scrawny birds started fighting. Heru knew they had no place showing up at our party."

"Shut up," Ginelle said. "Weren't you the only one who threw a punch? Besides, you know everyone is invited. Ginelle wanted Ty to calm down. His anger could easily stir more confusion. Confusion is what started the fight at the party and it got out of line quickly. New memes coming out every day was making it worse.

She wasn't even in the room when she heard one kid say to another that the falcons announced their fire before it even happened. Something about their school colors appearing. She was confused then, but everyone had seen the video now. Someone announced who at the party were falcons. There were only a few of them there. They probably didn't even go to the game or had left before the game even ended. When Ginelle ran into the room, Ty had just punched a Falcon in his Jaw. She could see a red, blue and yellow shirt rushing out the door. Third was quickly rushing towards the rest of the Falcons. "Take that shit outside," she yelled as soon as she realized what was going on. The last thing she needed was her house getting trashed. Her parents knew that she was hosting the party and although they were out with their own alumni friends, they would show up at the house at any time. They were down for the cause, but not for their house being destroyed. Ty yelled at all the Falcons to leave but she was nervous about them starting a fight in her yard. She heard sirens.

"I think the police knew where the party was," Darryl offered.

"Ha," Joey laughed, "That's no coincidence. Everybody knew where the party was." Ginelle watched as Joey twirled a pen between his fingers. "I'm sorry about that, Ginelle. I know how long you've been waiting to host a Panther party."

He was right. Since Ginelle's freshman year, she wanted to be a party host. She loved going to parties, but she loved entertaining more. She had a custom black and gray balloon arch made at her home's entrance. Inside there was a sweets table with black and gray wrapped cupcakes, cake balls, Oreos with gray frosting, the whole nine. She had to get really creative because most candies that were black in color didn't taste well. She found a way around that by wrapping most of the sweets in black or gray cellophane. Her backyard was the true coup de grace. To make sure that's where the true party happened, that's where the DJ was.

Her pool was covered with a dancefloor made of gray tinted glass. She had cocktail tables draped in black and gray with 16 inch Black Panther characters as the centerpieces. There was T'Challa,

Kilmonger, Nakia, Okoye, Shuri, Ramonda and even M'Baku.

She was so excited when she got the approval of the football and basketball captains earlier that year. That's all you needed. If they told the school what party they were going to, then that's the party everyone went to. There were parties all year, but to host one of the parties before or after the football and basketball rivalry, you were guaranteed to have a packed house. And you were guaranteed local celebrity status by both schools, especially if your party outshined another one.

The school's took turns. If the panthers hosted the pre basketball game party, the falcons would host the basketball game after party. Then the two would switch for the football game. The rivalry was more than just two separate teams. It was Hollywood within their city. It was everything. There was no need to destroy a legacy that two amazing schools had built.

"Aren't you missing something?" Darryl looked at Joey twirling the pen in his hand. Ginelle realized what he was referring to. You never saw Joey without his lighter. That's what he normally twirled through his fingers.

"Yea, talk about coincidences," Joey sighed. "My school gets burned down, my best friend gets burned up and I lose my lighter all in the same night," he shook his head and looked at the pen twirling between his fingers.

Ginelle, Ty and Darryl looked to each other at the same time. They all seemed to be thinking the same thing. *That is one hell of a coincidence.*

9 SUPERINTENDENT ANNOUNCEMENT

Dear district students, staff, teachers and community,

By now you have heard about the incident that occurred after our highly anticipated district high school football game, Heru vs Newton on Friday night. Immediately following the football game, highly flammable foam covered the front of the school and was set afire. This fire resulted in the injury of several students and significant damage to the Huey P. Newton High Schools' building and grounds. It is suspected that this act was part of an ongoing rivalry between the two schools.

At this time, we do not know who is responsible, but rest assured, the entire city is working together to get to the bottom of this. Please refrain from speculation as we allow the authorities time and space to do their jobs. Your energy is best spent in uplifting our injured students and their families and friends. The district is also working diligently towards the rebuilding efforts for Huey P. Newton high school. An attack such as this one, to a pillar in our community, is an attack on us all. We must work together as a community to uplift our injured students and Huey P. Newton High.

Because of this horrible act and the speculation and rumors surrounding it, all competitive activities within the district will be suspended until further notice. This includes all sports, debates, arts, or similar activities. In this time, we should gather as a community and leave the rivalry behind us.

Below you will find embedded links if you want to help our affected families or are in need of district supplied counseling. We have also added the contact information for the investigator handling the case, if you have any information that could assist the authorities in their investigation.

Our district will be one team and we will come out of this crisis stronger than ever before.

Dr Grant Smith

10 LANDON ELMORE

Landon was delirious. How did his son get caught up in this high school rivalry mess. He had already had two surgeries and had been in a coma for three days. The doctors did not seem optimistic. Keldon wasn't like his dad. He didn't play any sports. He wasn't even into the whole school rivalry thing, so Landon couldn't understand how this happened.

He wiped the tear that was forming in his eye. Every time he looked at those machines breathing for his son, it made his eyes well. He tried to be strong for his wife, but it wasn't working. He had to bribe her to go home. He wanted her to get some rest. He told her they needed some home cooked food and maybe the smell would remind Keldon of home while he slept. It was bullshit, but she bought it. He made her promise to lie down first, hoping it would help calm her. He thought without the sound of the machines and maybe if she felt the softness of their bed, it may force her to sleep. He could only hope.

They had talked to Keldon right before the fire. It was like his wife knew something might happen. They had only stopped by the alumni watch party for a second. They were at the bar just long enough to see the halftime show.

"Oh no, honey, do you think they're starting these pranks back up?" His wife asked with her eyes glued to the TV. The falcon was taking off his jersey.

"I hope not," he had urged. He had seen the video of his old friend yelling at Grant. He wished he hadn't said that or that it wasn't recorded. Everything Corbin had said was true, but he knew that was just enough to add fire to the friendly rivalry. He was there three years ago at that basketball game when the riot started. He was shocked no one died then. That was the perfect excuse for him to use for his son not to participate in any type of competitive sports at his alma mater.

He played football with Corbin back in high school. Corbin was a star. Everyone knew the panther's most accurate quarterback. Landon was a year younger and hardly received any playing time, but he loved being on the team and being recognized as a player on one of the best teams in the district. The panthers and falcons got along so well back then. The only time he remembered any tension was the year Grant threw all those interceptions. That was an exciting game for the panthers. The Falcons were pissed. The Panthers whole football team joked about how Jesse Jr. was able to destroy his father's legacy in one game.

"This is war," a Heru fan yelled from the bar. Everyone in the bar laughed and mingled while waiting for the third quarter. This is the rivalry he remembered when he was a panther. As a matter of fact, everything was friendly until after Dodge's party.

That's when he noticed his wife remove her phone from her ear. She turned to him and asked, "Honey, are you ready to go?"

"Is everything okay?" He asked as they walked to the car.

"Yea," I just tried Keldon. He didn't answer, so I'm going to call him back.

He couldn't believe she was hounding him. Then, he thought, she should be happy that he actually did something social instead of being locked in his room behind a computer screen. "Babe, can you imagine hanging out with your friends and your girlfriend at the most popular game of the year and then telling them, hold on, let me talk to my mom?"

"You're right," she laughed. "I just got a weird feeling."

"You're probably just a little anxious," he told her. It wasn't the first time she said something like that. She had a weird feeling several times a year and it was always nothing. It was always nothing, until that day.

Keldon called her back a few minutes later. She answered his call on speaker.

"Hey babe, are you having fun?" She answered.

"How'd that get there?" He asked.

"What's that?" she questioned.

"Oh, nothing mom. I'm fine. I'm about to meet Joey and Zandrea back at the bleachers."

He remembered looking over at his wife when he said that. She had rolled her eyes. She didn't like his girlfriend. It wasn't just that she was a falcon, they tried not to get wrapped up in the rivalry like the rest of the city. It was because she was rude and seemed so controlling. It didn't help that the more she complained, the closer they seemed to get. She learned not to say anything mean about his girlfriend when Keldon was in earshot.

"I bet y'all won't be saying that in a few months," a guy yelled into the phone.

"We ain't scared of y'all," another guy boasted.

"Ooh," Keldon muttered. They heard what sounded like a shuffle.

"Honey, is everything okay?" His wife was concerned.

"The athletes are trying to see who's nuts are bigger," Keldon joked.

"Don't use that language in front of your mother," Landon charged.

"Sorry dad," Keldon laughed. "I'll see you guys later," he hung up.

His wife was so happy to hear his voice. Landon wiped his eyes again. What if that was the last time he heard his sweet boy laugh? He tried to not watch the news, but the old rivalry kept coming up. The one from when he was on the football team. A scandal that he thought was behind them.

He walked over to Keldon's bed. He was covered from head to toe in bandages. If he wasn't his dad, he wouldn't even know it was him. But he knew everything about Keldon. He knew how long his arms were, how he sounded when he breathed, the shape of his head. Little things that only a parent could recognize from seeing their child grow from a baby to a grown man. Keldon was taller than him. He was taller than all of the men in their family, but he lacked any muscular build. He had to have gotten that from his mom.

He wanted to touch his forehead, but he was scared that the slightest touch could cause his son pain. He didn't want to add to his pain. If he could, he would trade places with him. There's no way, a kid with so much promise should be fighting for his life. He wanted nothing more than to find out who did this. Who burned up his little boy?

The detective said they knew it was arson. There was a lighter found with partial prints. They found some new clues and were following up on a few leads. They swore that they'd have more details in a few days.

One of Keldon's doctors walked into the room. Landon straightened up and wiped his eyes. The edges of his eyes were raw from wiping them so much. He looked into her eyes for signs of good news. He didn't see any.

"I don't have an update on his status. He's still stable, but nothing new about that." Landon waited patiently for her to continue. "We did just discover something that I wanted to share with you right away. We were really concerned with why Keldon's condition was so severe. More severe than the other students we have seen. We sent some fragments to the lab and we just received the results."

Landon didn't know why, but he returned to his seat. He knew he was just about out of energy and the last thing he needed was to fall in his son's hospital room. He was supposed to be strong for his family, but that was increasingly becoming impossible.

The doctor continued, "It appears, Keldon was wearing acrylic fabric," she moved her arms while she thought of what to say next. "It's popular in fall and winter clothing. It's lightweight but warming against the cool temperatures." Landon was confused. He didn't understand why she was talking about fashion. "It's also highly flammable," she added.

Landon's hand found his mouth. "He was wearing flammable clothing in a fire?" He asked to be sure that he understood her. She nodded. Landon thought back to that day. Friday when his son left the house. He wore black and gray. They all wore black and gray. He distinctly remembered that. It was a long sleeve T-shirt. "Acrylic?" He questioned aloud.

The doctor nodded. She was giving him time to process the information she had just given him.

"The fire marshal determined that there was a highly flammable foam that ignited the school. They call it elephant toothpaste. If Keldon was anywhere near those flames, there wasn't much he could do to avoid this accident." She curled the sides of her mouth up. She was trying to give him a comforting smile. He didn't feel comforted. "I just wanted to keep you informed."

"Thank you doctor," he responded.

"Do you need anything right now? Have you been to the cafeteria or would you prefer that we bring you something?"

"No thanks."

The doctor left. Landon knew something was off, but he couldn't put a finger on it. His eyes moved around the room as he tried to figure it out. He thought about that night. Big game days made everyone pull out their favorite school clothing. Every year he bought the family the latest Panther gear. This year, it was black and gray raglan shirts with a panther on it. His stomach churned as he thought about giving his son a highly flammable shirt that caused him to ignite in flames.

He remembered that he still had his shirt with him. He jumped up quickly as he thought about where he had last placed it. He hadn't been home since that night. The night of the game when they found out that Keldon was in the hospital. They heard about the fire and got scared when he didn't answer. His wife immediately called the hospital where the injured were taken. They confirmed that he had been admitted. He changed out of that T-shirt with one he had in the car just the day before.

He spotted his bag in the corner of the room. He snatched it up quickly and opened it. He had to confirm what the doctor said was true. He always thought those shirts were made of cotton or polyester. Who would think to look at the label of a promo shirt? He fished the black and gray shirt from his bag and turned to the label. What he found only confused him further. The label read, 100% cotton.

11 COLBY BRIDGES

The videos and memes were convincing, but Colby didn't think Mr. Dossani was responsible for the fire. Although if he was he had a good enough reason. At least it would mean that he finally grew a pair. It would mean that he finally stopped saying dumb shit, like let bygones be bygones and turn the other check and whatever other sayings people used to hide behind the fact that they were pure cowards.

They were the laughingstock of the city. How was it that 80 percent of the kids who were hurt in that fire were panthers? Colby had to make sure that the falcons would pay. Heru wouldn't get the last laugh in his last year. He'd see to it.

He had learned from that mascot prank that he didn't need to recruit people to help. Especially now that the stakes were so high. Even the teachers were encouraging the kids not to pull pranks and saying that the rivalry had gone too far. Yea, they could end all the rivalry talk as long as the last prank was pulled on the Falcons.

He came up with the mascot idea by himself after walking with his girlfriend after her cheer practice.

"Why y'all keep dancing to the same song over and over?" he asked her.

"That's our dance for the halftime show," Karissa responded.

"Y'all gotta dance to it every day? Don't that get boring?"

"Yea, but it's going to be so worth it when you see it all together on the field. We'll start practicing with the band next week, so we gotta make sure it's tight."

"Since when y'all practice with the band?"

She rolled her eyes at him. "How else do you think we're all doing the same routine on the field?"

Colby never gave it much thought. He had been to a million football games and never once wondered why they had the best band in the district. It was just something they did. "So y'all all gone be dancing to that song?"

She laughed at him. Colby looked at her until she answered. She must have thought he was joking. "On the field, the band is going to actually play the song that we were dancing to. It's not just us. The dancers and the color guard also practice separately. There's a few choreographed pieces that we do together, but we'll start perfecting that next week."

"Y'all better be careful. The Falcons might learn your routine," he said it as a joke, but got the idea while she was laughing. What if they pulled a prank during the halftime performance?

He started watching the band practice with their mascot. Of course the mascot didn't wear the panther costume during practice, but he didn't need to. Everyone knew who wore that costume.

"What are you guys doing when you lean back like that?" Colby asked Karissa after band practice that next week.

She was excited to tell him the entire plan. The band was going to split on two sides of the field, creating an aisle. Someone would carry a huge poster of a falcon attached to a long pole. The entire band would pretend to spit on the poster right before the two sides ripped it apart.

"I can't wait to see that," Colby said to her. He knew he would find a way to infiltrate that show. If they thought a poster was funny, what would they think about the actual mascot?

Colby was still mad about that basketball game last spring. He just knew that someone from Heru was trying to get him back for kissing their girl. Someone was playing with the scoreboard. He knew it was Heru and not simply a malfunction before the banner even dropped. He knew before halftime. He complained to the ref. He had to have lost half of his points, but no one wanted to listen to him.

"We have a whole camera crew in the stadium," he complained to Coach Robinson that night.

"We won the game, Colby. I'm sorry if you didn't get all of your points, but it's over. You still managed to get the most points on the team."

It was the principle of the thing and no one seemed to understand that. He was robbed. The refs didn't care, his teammates understood, but they didn't care either. He couldn't even get a copy of the game from the news station. He didn't know how and he didn't know when , but he knew he was going to get the Falcons back.

He had finally found his chance. The Huey P. pranks weren't huge, orchestrated plans. They were random pranks by random sports teams. He had even heard of the chess team pulling a prank at one of their chess tournaments by putting a strip of wet paint on Heru's team bench the morning of the tournament.

In the past, teachers and administrators would always threaten to take away playing time, so the students learned early not to speak about a prank, identify a prank or plan a prank aloud. The less you knew, the better. Pranks were to be enjoyed, not to be shared.

Colby couldn't pull this prank alone and he couldn't make a mistake. Thousands would watch the Panther vs Falcon football game. He recruited two of his teammates to help him. One that he knew had a cousin that played at Heru High and the other was a fearless thief.

When the three of them were alone, he started picking their brains.

"Do y'all ever think about getting the Falcons back for that basketball game?"

"All the time," Kedric responded.

Colby smiled. He could tell by Kedric's facial expression that he was dead serious. "I got an idea," he said.

He only told them that he needed to steal the falcon's mascot so that it couldn't make it on the field during game day. He would hold it for safekeeping until the game was over. Darryl was able to figure out where the mascot was stored while Kedric was able to figure out how to retrieve it without being seen. It was about time Darryl proved himself worthy.

They met in the gym the afternoon before the game. They were almost caught by Coach Robinson. He was cool with them, but something told Colby that he was not to be trusted. Most transplants didn't understand the rivalry between the teams.

Colby took the mascot home and tried it on. He wanted to make sure everything was perfect. He was excited that he was finally going to get his revenge. He fantasized about the memes that would circulate after he pulled off the most epic prank ever.

Colby had almost changed his mind about his plan twice. The first time was when he put the falcon head on. That thing stunk. What did people do to it? Was it onions? Must? Halitosis? He sprayed way too much Febreze inside and put it to the side also. He was about to put the Febreze back then thought better of it. He sprayed the inside of the body cavity and sat it to the side. He picked up the feet and examined them. He could tell that they were way too small.

"What am I doing?" he asked himself before dropping the foot to the floor. He could just see those falcons laughing as he got angrier and angrier that their scoreboard was wrong. He couldn't even focus on his game from watching the scoreboard. "See, it's wrong again," he had yelled. Colby picked up the falcon's foot. He sprayed the inside of it as well.

It took him an hour to get the mascot uniform to smell to his liking and stretch to his size. He had to cut slits through the feet so that he could wear them. He stopped by a party store to buy one of those all over spandex suits. He chose the color yellow because it seemed to match with the Falcon's head and feet. The suit would help camouflage the fact that the bird was entirely too small.

He wore the spandex suit under his clothes and waited for halftime. He responded to a few texts to make it seem like he was always available. It was easy to lose friends at a football game.

Colby was shocked to see the Heru falcon performing in their halftime show. He looked back into the bag to make sure it wasn't his bird out dancing in the middle of the field. It wasn't. His bird was sitting right next to him. He never thought they would have more than one costume. It was just like the Falcons to have back up plans on top of back up plans. Colby was even more excited to pull his prank. Just before the Panther mascot was to run out onto the field, Colby ran up to him in full uniform to tell him there would be a change of plan. When the panther saw his toes hanging out of the Falcon's feet, it was obvious that this was part of a prank.

The mascots fed off of each other's energy. It was epic. Colby simply left the bird in the bag by the bleachers when it was all said and done. He took his clothes from his backpack and dressed right there behind the bleachers. He blended in with the rest of the students in black and gray. He couldn't stop smiling when he caught up with his friends. It was probably the best prank ever, until of course the falcons burned down their school. Colby decided that he would exchange fire for fire. Heru wasn't getting the last laugh again. He'd make sure of that.

He parked down the street from Heru high. He noticed a security guard standing near the entrance. Standing near the very thing he was planning to ignite. He had to get the security officer away from the 12 foot falcon. It looked like a parade float. Colby guessed that it was made out of shiny plastic. *That will probably burn easily,* he smiled.

He looked around for an opportunity. He didn't want to stand out there too long by himself. Someone could see him and think he was suspicious. One security officer was just enough to say you were protecting the school on paper, but the reality was that anyone could outrun one guy. Especially a middle aged, out of shape one who carried nothing but a flashlight.

A gleam caught the corner of Colby's eye. A silver Porsche just past the security officer, parked in front of the school. A car like that had to have a nice alarm system. Colby guessed that the car was twenty feet away from him and between him and the car was the security officer. The officer wasn't focused. He was laughing at something on his phone.

Colby looked around the bush he was behind for something to throw. All those long shots he had practiced over the years, twenty feet was nothing. He spotted a pebble, but it was too small. He continued his search until he heard voices. He peered over the bush. Damn. The Porsche's owner was walking out of the school. And the security officer was now at high alert. He was walking around, looking. Two sets of eyes were worse than one. Colby knew that he should abort mission. His chances of getting caught were increasing. He could always try again the next day. But how would he distract the security guard then? What if there were more security guards? What would he do?

The Porsche owner turned to wave at the security officer before sliding into his car. That's when Colby saw his face. He had seen it on the news all week, so there was no denying it. It was Mr. Smith, the superintendent. What was he doing at Heru high after dark? He hadn't visited Newton high once that Colby knew of and their school was the one burned up.

Wasn't Mr. Smith also a Heru Falcon? Colby remembered some of the students talking about some ancient rivalry that started between Mr. Dossani and Mr. Smith when they were in high school. The rumor was that they were the ones who started the school rivalry thing in the first place. *Just wait until people hear about this. Secret meetings with Heru?*

What was he thinking? Who would he tell? He would be incriminating himself. This secret meeting would have to be just that, a secret. The Heru Falcons would again have the last laugh. Colby decided right then and there, not on his watch. He unzipped his backpack as he watched the silver Porsche turn the corner. The security officer was near the spot that the Porsche had just left. He didn't have to pretend anymore. He looked at his phone on his walk back to his sitting post. Right next to the falcon.

Now or never. Colby lit the first Molotov and it landed right at the base of the falcon. He lit the second one quickly and it landed on top of the first one. The security officer was frozen in his tracks. Colby knew that he was probably in shock, but he couldn't wait around for him to come to his senses.

Colby jogged two blocks, put a yellow shirt on over his black one and walked into the fast food joint. He was sure that the falcon was already nothing but wire. He chewed his taco while watching the speeding fire truck through the restaurant window. At least their bird sat alone on top of concrete. Their school was safe.

"Hello," he answered his buzzing phone while continuing to chew.

"Bro, did you hear? Someone burned down the Heru Falcon."

He slurped the last sip of his coke through the straw. "Wow. That's crazy."

12 CORBIN DOSSANI

If it wasn't one thing it was another. Corbin thought about retiring, but he knew the school district required at least another two decades before it was even considered. Maybe he could switch careers. But what would he do? He had only been an educator. Maybe he'd be able to skip states. Surely every district couldn't be this stressful.

Corbin thought he was going to sleep early. He thought sleep could erase some of the stress of his school being burned down. Of this stupid rivalry that had continued all these years. How could a rivalry continue so long? He was physically tired. The Sandman hadn't visited him since the football game. Since his school's entrance turned into ash.

He had just been alerted that the falcon in front of Heru High school no longer existed. It disintegrated in flames. Another case of arson.

Corbin didn't want to worry, but he knew his students would be blamed for it even though the security guard didn't see anything. Who else would burn up their school staple, but someone from Huey P?

Corbin knew it shouldn't have been his first thought, but he made the call anyway.

"Ay what's up Corbin."

"I need to ask you a favor, but I'm not really asking. I never called."

"Anything," Dodge answered. "Power to the People."

"Power to the Panthers," Corbin replied. "I just found out the falcon was set afire. I have no idea who did it, but Huey should probably have round the clock protection. This shit's getting out of hand and after all he's been through, he can't suffer in this mess. I don't know how long it's going to take for this thing to get sorted out." It was bad enough Corbin had to find out that a zippo lighter was found at the scene of his school's fire from a news station. And of all stations, it was a channel 8 exclusive. They favored Heru, so no telling where they had gotten that information from. He was still waiting for the fire marshal to call him back to confirm.

"Consider it done."

"Bet." They hung up. If Corbin could trust anyone to protect their beloved statue of Huey P. Newton, it was Dodge. It was his idea to have the statue put up in the first place. They wanted to honor the hero at their school. It was their class gift.

After the release of the global blockbuster movie, *Black Panther*, the students came up with a bright idea of their own senior gift. Panthers cut out of bushes, flanking the entrance of the school. Corbin thought the idea was okay but didn't take them seriously until they came up with the designs and the money. Corbin hated that they went in the fire. He knew how much the kids loved them. But the alumni felt the same way about the Huey P. Newton statue. The alumni knew that Huey P. Newton was the sacred jewel of the school. Everyone respected Huey, but after recent events, Corbin wasn't so sure that people would remember that. The city seemed to have lost their minds.

People were actually taking sides. People blamed Heru High as they should have, since their colors were what set the school afire, but people were also blaming him. They thought he would actually burn down his very own school. Who could be that desperate to burn down their own school? To put his students, his staff and his alumni in danger. To put the students, staff and alumni of Heru high in danger. He had even heard they were trending. He hated that hashtag, epic school prank. He wasn't fond of Grant, but he didn't hate anyone that much.

He and Grant were once good friends. Almost best friends. Had they gone to the same school they likely would have been. They went to the same elementary and middle school, but parted ways in high school. Their friendship is what made the schools so close. It birthed their friendly rivalry. It started their tradition of alternating team parties that morphed into school parties. Students from both schools once went to every one of their games as if they attended both schools. It was friendly competition, but in their senior year, everything changed.

Corbin and Grant were both quarterbacks of their football teams. What was once a pregame party for just the football team, turned into a pregame party for the football, basketball, baseball and soccer teams. More people showed up than had ever before. That must have been what inflated Grant's ego. That must have been what made him think he should drink that night.

"I got people coming in from out of town to watch you, Grant," one of Heru's basketball player's boasted. "Don't embarrass me."

"Consider yourself embarrassed, because my boy is going to show out," Dodge bragged. The teams had stuffed inside of the Dodge's house. The guys were hanging around the grill talking.

"There's going to be so many people at this game tomorrow. Even the mayor is talking it up," Corbin said. "I'm getting nervous. Everyone and I mean everyone from the school has said they'll be there."

"We've been getting the same vibes at Heru. This could be the biggest game in the state."

Corbin remembered Grant drinking from a red cup. It was the third drink he had. Someone passed him a fourth one. "Ay, you may want to slow down on those," Corbin told Grant in a loud whisper.

"Don't worry," Grant boasted, "I'll still have enough energy to destroy y'all tomorrow," Corbin smiled at Grant's slurred speech. He stood up. "I'm going to gone and head home. I need to rest before the big game. Do you need a ride?" He knew that Grant had driven, but he wanted to give him an out if he needed one. If he didn't want his ego bruised by leaving early or drinking less.

"Nah, I'm good," he uttered.

"Alright guys," I'll see you at the after party tomorrow. Corbin left. He didn't know how much longer the guys partied. He didn't know if Grant left soon after or stayed to have more drinks, but if his memory served him right, he thought, Dodge, had told him that Grant was one of the last people to leave.

No athlete in their right mind would drink the night before a big game. And even if they were dumb enough to indulge, they wouldn't have more than one. Grant was sloppy on the field the next day. It was hard to say who would have won the game if he was sober, but he definitely played against himself in that game.

Grant threw not one, not two, but three interceptions during the game. Everyone knew how fast the panther's defense was then. Not even an amateur quarterback would throw those flimsy passes. It was obvious that Grant didn't bring his A game. He didn't bring his B through D game either.

Corbin remembered feeling bad for him. He should have been celebrating his perfect passes and wise decisions on the field that day, but instead he was thinking about his friend. He knew the coach had to have attacked him each time he stepped off the field. His teammates looked at him in disappointment. It got so bad that the coach had to pull him out in the fourth quarter. Their second stream, who had never played in a varsity game had to step in for him. And although he was bad, he managed to complete more passes than Grant.

Grant wouldn't make eye contact with him after the game. He wouldn't answer Corbin's calls either. Corbin thought he just needed time until he caught wind of the rumor. According to the Falcons, the Panthers drugged their football players at the pregame party. Corbin was confused. Was this something that happened after he left the party? Wait, what was he thinking?

He called Grant again. This time leaving him a message. "I'm just checking on you. I hope you're feeling better .Ay, have you heard anything about this rumor going around? It's crazy that some of your teammates think you were drugged at Dodge's house. I want to know where this rumor got started. It's weird. Anyway, holla back."

That was Corbin's last time reaching out to him. It was clear that he wouldn't return any of his calls. It was crystal clear when he saw him after graduation. He was hanging with some of his teammates at the local diner. Corbin stopped by their table to speak and was ignored. There had to be at least five other football players there talking to each other like Corbin wasn't standing right next to them. Corbin finally walked away, thinking he may have been tripping until he turned back to see Grant's smirk. Their wide receiver, JJ, had his arm around him. He had to have been whispering something about Corbin because they both looked his way.

He didn't see Grant again after that. Not until it was announced that he was the new superintendent. The new superintendent who acted like the same lying, over inflated, ego driven, narcissist that he was as a high school senior.

The video that Renae's brother posted from the school board meeting showed when he was upset and yelling at Grant, but it didn't show what happened before that. What seemed to slip everyone's mind soon after.

Grant sat in the front of the room, seated next to the other school board members. Below them sat an audience full of school administrators, teachers and parents. Grant made an announcement explaining how the recent bond money would be allocated throughout the district. It was obvious that Huey P.'s school renovations were missing from the list. Corbin casually made his way to the nearest mic so that he would have a chance to present his question to the board.

"In the list you just read, I didn't hear anything about the renovations that need to be made at Huey P. Newton high school."

"That's correct," Grant responded.

"Did you forget to read that line? Is it on another list?" Corbin was confused.

"No," Grant said flatly.

"We'll have to revisit school renovations at a later time," Grant's old friend, JJ responded. He was on the board longer than Corbin could remember. That's when it dawned on Corbin that he must've gotten Grant the job in the first place. He was a legacy man and would ensure that Heru's interests were first. Corbin could feel his blood start to boil.

Grant busied himself looking at the paper that was in front of him and talking with JJ. It was just like that day in the diner. Here Corbin was, standing in front of him, in front of a mic and Grant acted like he didn't exist. That wouldn't bother Corbin if he wasn't the only person who could truthfully answer the question he had.

Corbin lost it right then. Coincidentally it was the same time Renae started recording. "This is some stupid rivalry shit isn't it?" he accused. Grant heard that because he was now looking Corbin directly in his eyes. "How come Heru just got their basketball gym resurfaced and a new bird in front of their school?" Corbin chose his words carefully, he knew that Falcons didn't like to be called birds. "You know what? While we're here Grant, why don't you tell these people the truth. There is no rivalry. You started a rumor because you drank too much the night before the game. You played like shit. Tell the district, shame the devil."

"Mr. Dossani, please leave the mic," JJ called. "Someone please remove his mic," he repeated.

Grant didn't speak. He just stared for a second and then a faint smirk appeared on his face. He returned to busying himself pretending to read the paper before him.

"Tell these people. You failed your team. You were never a dedicated player. If Heru wants to start a rivalry, they need to start one with you." Corbin was yelling now because someone removed his mic.

"Corbin, do we have to have security remove you or can you act civilized like the rest of the audience?" JJ said.

"It's your fault these kids are pranking each other for some stupid rivalry that never happened. Because you lied to your team. You lied to your city. Tell the truth, Grant." That part wasn't heard on the video because Corbin was too far away from the mic. He noticed security walking toward him so he put his hands up in surrender and pretended to walk back to his seat. Security began to walk back to where they had come from.

Corbin couldn't resist the mic that was almost given to another audience member. He snatched it right before the audience member could grasp it. "Mark my words," he accused. "My kids will get their school improvements by any means necessary." With that, he left the room. He didn't want to be escorted out by security.

Corbin didn't mean to get so upset, but he had worked on those renovations for his school for years. Corbin had lobbied for renovations of Huey P. High since he became principal five years before. It was what he had promised the alumni, students, parents and staff. He had no intention of not delivering his promise. The previous superintendent explained that they just didn't have the funds.

Three years ago, the idea for this bond was addressed at a school board meeting. Corbin made sure to remind the superintendent of his promise, and he was assured that Huey High would not be forgotten. It took another year for the bond to be on the ballot. It took two more years for the funds to come available. This happened right before the superintendent announced his retirement.

Never in a million years did Corbin think the transition from one superintendent to the next would cause his school to lose much needed rehabilitation funding. He was shocked to see Grant make a return to the district, but if that was the guy the school board chose, that must have meant that he was qualified. Corbin never thought about a school rivalry.

After that outburst, Corbin felt personally responsible for making sure his students didn't feel a need to retaliate. Especially when he realized that one of his favorite employees had exposed him. He thought they were on the same page. He was making a statement by hiring a Heru Falcon to his staff. She was making a statement by becoming the cheerleading coach. He knew the rivalry was untrue and silly, so he never thought that a plea to stop the pranks would backfire.

He wanted to be petty like everyone else, but he had a student dying in the hospital behind this stupid rivalry. Someone had to be the adult, even if the leader of the entire school district wouldn't.

13 DR. GRANT SMITH

Grant could tell that Corbin was out for blood, but he just didn't know how far he would go. Could he really have been capable of burning his own school down to prove a point? Corbin always did think he was the most moral person.

Sure, Grant made a few mistakes as a kid, but he was a responsible adult now. He wanted nothing more than to be a leader for everyone in his district, especially the kids of his alma mater, Heru. When JJ called him to present him with the job, he had to think on it long and hard. Did he really want to return to the district? It was the most embarrassing thing that had ever happened to him.

JJ reminded him that it was an opportunity for him to change his legacy. He owed it to Heru to do something good for them, especially when he caused them to be the laughingstock of the city twenty years before. It was a good opportunity. Grant decided to take it. It wasn't like he really had a choice.

Though he was happy to see some familiar faces, he was quickly reminded of his past. School board members from Heru often told him to do what was right. By what was right, they meant to do what was right by Heru. Their school was named after the ancient, virgin born god of Egypt. The god of kingship and of the sky. From his name came the word hero. It only made sense that those who considered themselves Heru Falcons would be of the elite. There was once a legacy there, and Grant was guilted into thinking he had been the one to destroy that legacy.

That night, twenty years ago at the pre-game party was a blur to Grant. He remembered being frustrated. That was the night he found out his mom had cancer. His dad was moving the family after graduation to be near the best cancer center in the country. He hadn't told anyone yet. He didn't know how to feel.

Grant had already figured out his graduation plans. He chose a partial scholarship to play football at one of the state schools. Partial because he didn't want the football program to own him. He definitely wanted to play, but he had academic goals too. He knew then that he wanted to go into education. He had his eye on being a superintendent at 17. His father told him that this diagnosis changed everything for their family, including his future. As the oldest of five children and being a new adult, he had to stay behind to help. Cancer wasn't cheap.

He went to the pre-game party that night thinking that being around friends would help him forget his situation, at least temporarily. Every now and then, he would forget about the cancer but it was still a dark cloud hovering above him. He could hear the thunder and was just waiting for the rain to fall. He had never drank before but saw a few players drinking beer. He figured, *what could it hurt?* That was the first of a string of bad decisions.

He was a selfish son. He didn't know the severity of the situation, but cancer never sounded good. People died from that. A lot of people died from that. Did that mean that his mother would die? His mother was full of life. She was the backbone of the family. They would not survive without her. There was no way his father could take care of them by himself. He didn't even know how to cook, when the bills were due, or how to keep his youngest sister's asthma from flaring up.

His dad appeared to have aged ten years when he told him the news. He knew something was wrong when he walked into his office. He thought maybe he had lost his job or something. That would be bad, but his dad was brilliant. He could find another. When his dad looked up at him, he knew it was something more. Grant was the first person his dad told. His siblings didn't even know yet. Like Grant, they thought she was visiting family for a few days.

His dad had already gone into fix-it mode. He had just discovered the cancer center. After comparing it to regular chemo and the local cancer centers, he learned that it had the highest success rate. The fee was going to cost another mortgage, but Grant knew that his dad would go bankrupt if he thought it could save his mom.

Grant was being selfish. He was thinking about missing out on college and missing out on football while his mom was literally dying. What kind of son was he? He was an ungrateful one. Grant wanted something stronger. Someone passed him a red cup.

"Ay man, you may want to slow down," Corbin had told him.

Grant remembered looking at Corbin with anger. He didn't have to make any adult decisions. His biggest worry was the next football game. Maybe which college he'd choose. He was waiting until the last minute to decide. He didn't know anything about adult decisions. "Nah, I'm good," he told him.

Grant got up to go to the bathroom. He saw Dodge's dad. "Hey, what's up boy," he called to him. He was smoking a cigar.

Grant walked into his office. "Hey Mr. Dodge, I didn't know you were here."

"You didn't think I was going to leave you kids without a chaperone, did you? And piss off all your parents?"

Grant had always heard that parents were at the parties but he had never seen them, so he figured that was a lie people told so other parents wouldn't worry. "No, you're right."

"Are you ready for this big game tomorrow?"

"Yea." Grant wasn't worried about the game. He could complete passes in his sleep and everyone in the city knew it. People had been following him since he was in little league.

"I know you are," Mr. Dodge laughed. "I got a lot of money riding on this game. If you feel like overthrowing a few passes, some of us won't be mad at you." He smiled.

"What do you mean?" Grant took two more steps into his office.

"I dabble a little bit with numbers. I had to put something on my boy," he lowered his voice, "don't tell anyone about that though."

"So you bet on us? On the game?"

"Yea. It's not that unusual. I bet on a lot of things?"

"Do you win money?"

"Sometimes. Sometimes, I lose. I never bite off more than I can chew." He took a puff of his cigar. "Some people drink. Some cheat. Some drugs. I gamble."

Of course, Grant knew what gambling was, but he didn't know anyone who gambled outside of Vegas. He didn't know people gambled on football games. He didn't know people gambled on his football games. He could use a few dollars to help his dad. He had at least $1,000 in his savings account, but cancer would laugh at that amount. "How much could I win if I put money on the game? Say… $1,000."

"Whoa, youngster. I wouldn't recommend that. Gambling is a dangerous sport. It can become expensive, too."

"I just want to do it once. I need some money." He knew he sounded desperate, but he didn't care. It took him months to save that money, but he couldn't afford any more months. His family needed money now. He didn't know how to rob or steal, so that was out of the question. Besides, if cancer didn't kill his mom, him going to jail would surely do it. This sounded easy. And he could win the game on his worst day.

Mr. Dodge looked serious. "Close the door, young man."

Grant complied. In less than two minutes, he got a crash course on betting odds. "So, I'd make more money if we lost the game?"

"Yea, but you don't want to do that. We want to see real competition out there."

He was getting frustrated. Mr. Dodge was not listening to him. "I just need some money right now. I can't explain it, but I promise you it's just this one time."

Mr. Dodge was stern. "Maybe there's something else I could do. I could give you a loan-"

"No," Grant interrupted him. His dad was a proud man. He watched his dad struggle when he was a kid. All he had to do was ask his grandfather for some money, but he wouldn't. "My dad has enough problems." Grant looked at him, comfortably smoking his cigar. His family did well, but not as well as the Dodges. Mr. Dodge had just told him that he played with his money as a guilty pleasure. "How much did you put on the game?"

"Five grand," he exhaled.

"On a game that you knew you would lose?"

Mr. Dodge inhaled another puff before slowly exhaling a cloud of smoke. "Come on, Grant. You're good. You really are. But you're not the team. Your fullbacks leave you exposed all the time, causing you to run around the field more than you need to. Your star wide receiver is afraid to get tackled. Your star running back is recovering from an injury. I saw him in those last two games. He's out there running scared. He's not trying to get hurt again. And there's the fact that I would never ever bet against my boy. You guys are definitely favored, but I think I got a good shot. Besides, I like upsets. It's usually how I bet anyway. It really gets the blood flowing." He smiled.

Grant couldn't believe this man was playing with money like that. What kind of psychopath was he? "If I throw the game, will you give me some of your winnings?" Grant asked him.

Mr. Dodge stood up. "I don't want to be in the middle of anything like that. I'm sorry I gave you that idea. Go enjoy your party, son." He walked to the door.

Grant put his foot in front of the door to keep Mr. Dodge from opening it. "Please, Mr. Dodge. Can you promise me that if I help you, you'll share your winnings with me?"

"Son, if you need-"

"Please. Promise me."

Mr. Dodge sighed and threw up his hands. "Fine, but never ever talk to me about a game again. I don't meddle in kid affairs."

"I promise." Grant put his hand out, expecting a handshake.

Mr. Dodge looked at his hand. He frowned. Grant waved his extended hand in front of him. Showing him that he was still waiting. Mr. Dodge's brows pinched before he finally shook his head, then Grant's hand.

Grant showed up the next day when he knew everyone was at the Heru afterparty. Mr. Dodge let him inside his house but wouldn't let him sit down. "Wait here," he said. He came back with a thick envelope. Grant smiled. Mr. Dodge wore the same frown from the night before. He dropped the envelope in Grant's waiting hand. "I never want to hear anything about this again."

"You have my word." Grant thought about the cancer program fee that his dad was worried about. It could take months to sell their home. Now, he'd have to find a way to say this donation was anonymous. He hated what he did to his team, but saving his family was worth it.

After all these years, Grant still didn't regret his decision. His mom got better. His dad would probably be in debt for the rest of his life, but he was happy. They had to downgrade to a smaller house, his dad had to move to a less promising career, but his parents were still together and relatively healthy. They were happy. He made the sacrifice that a man was supposed to make.

When his friend, Greg, started the rumor, he didn't like it but it was better than the truth. "What happened? Were you drugged?" Greg had asked.

He thought it was a rhetorical question meant to make him feel bad, so he didn't respond.

"That's it, huh?" Greg assured, "They spiked that red cup you were drinking out of."

Grant didn't agree or deny. His silence was enough for Greg to run with the rumor. He didn't know if Greg was protecting Grant or himself. A few sloppy handoffs to Greg ended up being fumbles.

Everyone knew something was up with his game, but they didn't know what. It was true that he had a hangover the next day and he didn't play his best game, but those interceptions were intentional. He wanted Mr. Dodge to know that he had worked for his money. Grant's going away party at the diner was unsurprisingly thin. Only a handful of his friends still supported him after that embarrassing upset. His loyalty was being questioned. There was no way he'd be seen talking with a Panther. He knew Corbin wouldn't understand and he didn't care.

He did feel guilty about what he did. He was going to make it right every chance he got. Heru would finally be the best at more than just football and he was making sure of that, starting with improving some of the sports programs. It took a lot of creative engineering to ensure funds were allocated their way, and now the arson case was going to be an obstacle in his plans.

Heru colors before the fire was making them look like more than just bad guys. There was no way they would recover if the fire marshal wasn't also a Falcon. The inside information helped them to frame the story before they fed it to Channel 4. After the lighter was found at the scene of the arson, Grant rushed to look into the backgrounds of staff and students, and only one blemish belonging to the Panthers was worth leaking to the news.

JJ reminded him over and over that his job was to protect the image of Heru and he'd control the image of this case before any charges were filed. Now that a gold lighter was found at the scene, he was working with the principal of Heru to clear his students and staff before making it public. They didn't need to know the details, as long as it didn't tarnish the image of Heru. He was no investigator, but after the falcon in front of Heru went ablaze, he was certain this whole fiasco was one big arson case. That and the inscription the fire marshal showed him from that golden lighter:

Playing with fire is bad for those who burn themselves. For the rest of us, it is a very great pleasure. – Jerry Smith

14 AMARIS TUCKER

Amaris couldn't believe that Keldon was in the hospital. She wasn't close to him, but it really bothered Joey. If he had just stayed with them instead of his girlfriend, he would probably be okay. Joey never understood what Keldon saw in Zandrea. There were plenty of eligible girls at Huey P. Newton. This was a lesson to everyone that it was best not to date rivals. At least you didn't have to worry about if you could trust them. Amaris knew that firsthand.

Amaris never tried to get to know Zandrea. Knowing that she went to Heru was enough for her. The mood changed when they were around. She was laughing with Keldon and Joey when Zandrea showed up.

"What's that thing you keep twirling on your fingers.?" Amaris asked Joey.

"Noooo," Keldon started. "Don't ask him that." She looked up at Keldon as he spoke. His deep dimples dotted his medium brown cheeks before his smirk spread into a smile. That smile turned his eyes into slits that made them hard to see behind his black plastic frames. She couldn't figure him out. He looked like a geek and a jock.

"Well, I'm glad you asked." Joey smiled. He smiled at Keldon before flicking open the Zippo lighter. "Check this out." He turned on the flame and grabbed it with his other hand. The flame disappeared. He then snapped his other finger and the flame turned back on. He let it burn for a second before closing the lid. Now, Amaris understood that wasn't a birth mark on his hand, but a burn mark.

"Whoa, how did you do that?" Amaris asked.

"It's simple. I can show you," Joey said.

Keldon rolled his head back. "Here we go."

"Or how about this one?" Joey asked. He opened the lid and turned the flame back on. This time, he grabbed the flame and seemingly put it in his mouth. He blew his breath back onto the lighter and the flame reappeared.

"Wow," Amaris laughed. "Now that's cool."

"It's not that simple," Keldon said.

"Try it, try it, old man." Joey turned to Keldon.

"You know I can never do that. You're always trying to burn shit."

He turned to her. "Amaris, you have to try it. It's easy. Let me show you."

He did his first trick again. He put his finger over the flame and they watched it disappear. After his third try, she was finally convinced that it was easy enough for her to try. She took the lighter. "Ouch!" She dropped it.

"Come on... don't treat my equipment like that." Joey picked up the lighter and showed her the trick again. "You have to lightly grab the edge of the flame. You're trying to hold the damn thing." He explained as he slowly pulled his fingers over the base of the flame.

Amaris watched him carefully. "Well, of course it looks easier when you do it."

"I'm telling you. You can learn this trick in less than 60 seconds."

"Hey, baby," Keldon said. Both Amaris and Joey looked up to see who he was talking to. It was a girl wearing an ugly sweater.

"Where have you been?" the girl accused.

Joey straightened his posture and put his hands in his letterman. His face was annoyed. Amaris remembered the girl's extremely long braids from the pre-game party the night before. She knew then that she was Heru. At the party, she was with a couple of girls wearing cropped Heru hoodies and, of course, the braids were a dead giveaway.

"Hi to you, too." Joey held his head high as he looked down on her.

Zandrea did a once over of him and Amaris and quickly muttered, "Hi," before turning back to Keldon. "You were supposed to meet me by the concession stand."

"I was there for a while. You didn't show. I figured you got held up." Keldon smiled. "I tried calling you, but your phone's going to voicemail."

Amaris guessed that he was dating the girl. Her tense actions didn't faze him. He was just as calm as before. He smiled as he listened to her intently. Her attitude didn't deserve his patience.

"She was probably with her friend from last night," Joey scoffed.

The girl rolled her eyes at Joey before explaining, "My phone's dead. I was late because the sweaters were late."

Joey sighed, "Ay bro, we'll catch you in the stands. You are sitting on the Panthers' side, right?" Joey stared at Keldon, his face waiting for an affirmative answer.

Keldon smiled. "Of course." He then tapped Amaris on her arm and smiled at her. "It was nice meeting you."

Amaris smiled back but stopped when she saw the face his girlfriend gave her. Pyro wrapped his arm around Amaris's shoulder, forcing her to turn away.

"What's her problem?" Amaris asked Joey as they walked to the stands.

"She's a Heru bitch," Joey answered.

Amaris laughed. "I guess that explains it all."

She had talked to Joey a few times since that day and he wasn't taking it well. He kept saying that he warned Keldon about dating someone from Heru. He thought they should have stayed with Keldon that day. That he shouldn't have left him with that girl, but Amaris didn't know what he thought he could do. She didn't know what he thought the girl could have done to hurt him.

The rumors were always bad, but now they were outrageous. A new meme was created daily. Once those were shared, it was a wrap. Amaris saw one that said *you're cursed if you date someone from the rival school.* Now, people were saying it was a curse that hurt Keldon. There was one where someone photoshopped pictures of Heru cheerleader heads on chicken bodies. It said, *Never date a bird, they'll get you killed.*

There was a video of Keldon and Zandrea circulating online. It was posted on his page right before that fire happened. It took a while before his identification became public, so there was a delay in people finding the video. But once they did, the video had been morphed into hundreds of jokes and rival slander. People had taken that five-second video and turned it into hundreds of memes. Some were praying that he got better and claiming that the couple was happy, but most were vultures from both sides destroying the other. Amaris was down with the rivalry, but they sometimes took it too far.

The video must have been taken after Joey and Amaris left the two alone. They were dressed in matching ugly sweaters. The sweaters were in block colors. One side was black and gray and the other side was red, blue, and yellow. Now that Amaris had time to observe the sweater, she was pretty sure that it was supposed to show both sides coming together. *That's sweet,* she thought.

In the video, Keldon smiled at the camera. Zandrea giggled and said, "It's a video, silly, not a photo."

"Oh," he said, "well in that case-" He grabbed her face and kissed her on the lips. The video ended a second after that. It was posted on his page, but she was tagged in the video. There was no caption and no hashtags.

Amaris tried to read the comments, but they were horrible.

That's what happens when you date a Heru

You mean... that's what happens when you try to defile a Heru

She was obviously in on it. Falcons and Panthers can NEVER mix

It sounded harsh, but Amaris knew all too well about that. She sometimes felt guilty about the role she played in a failed Panther and Falcon romance. One of the Heru guys played her friend, so she decided to play a prank on him. Sometimes, she regretted it, but she was happy that no one knew that it was her.

Keianna seemed to be in love with Ron. Amaris didn't understand how since he always seemed too busy to hang out with her. One day, Keianna finally agreed to meet him at his house. According to

Keianna, nothing happened, but she was inconsolable after he blocked her the next day. He blocked her online as well. When she saw him at the basketball afterparty, he treated her like scum. He said that Panther girls were beneath him.

"I don't know what I did wrong," Keianna cried to Amaris after lunch one day.

"Are you serious? What you did wrong? Did he really throw that stupid rivalry in the middle of him being a jerk?"

"I was so embarrassed. His friends just looked at me and laughed." She wiped tears that were forming in her eyes. "Do you think all Heru guys are like that?"

"What?" Amaris stared into her eyes. She was looking to see if she had any sense left. "Are you thinking of dating more of them? Are you trying to find out?"

"No, I just…"

"Never date a Heru. And that Ron, he's going to get what's coming to him. Don't you worry."

Amaris didn't know what she meant by that, but she could feel the anger rising within her. She knew all of this only happened because Keiannna was so gullible. But that didn't give anyone the right to walk all over her. They saw her long, wavy hair and hazel eyes and thought she was gorgeous, but when they found out she was lovestruck, they abused her. She couldn't warn Keianna enough, but she figured out how to make Ron pay.

She stalked the two pages Ron had online. He actually had one for tennis and one for basketball. Such a jerk. She learned the type of girls he liked and what interested him and she became that girl when she had finally seen him at a team party. She didn't worry if her tamed locs, almond eyes, and full lips were attractive to him. She could tell he didn't have a physical type. He was more interested in behavior.

She flirted with him heavy until he finally exchanged phone numbers with her. She would text him every day telling him anything he wanted to hear. He kept asking to meet up with her, but she always had the perfect excuse. After weeks of pressure, she finally agreed to meet up with him, but there was one thing she needed to hear before she agreed. She sounded real thirsty, but he finally sent the right reply, *I'd rather be with a Panther.*

Bingo. She masked her number and forwarded it to Keianna within seconds. It was on Instagram in minutes. The guy swore that someone must've gotten his phone number and stole his images then photoshopped that message. The Panthers didn't care. They didn't let it die down for months.

Pranking was deceitful. She never wanted to get involved, but she hated how Ron made Keianna feel. The prank at least made Keianna happy. It had somehow boosted her self-esteem. She often had to convince herself that she did the right thing. With Keldon being injured the way he was, she may never be able to convince herself of that again.

"How's school going?" her mom asked as she put her phone on the kitchen island. Her mom must have read her face. "That bad, huh?"

She just shook her head as her mom gave her a hug. She didn't even know why she felt so bad. She didn't even know Keldon. She had only started hanging with Joey a few weeks before then. They weren't even dating, they were just hanging out. She couldn't tell how close he was with Keldon, but he didn't really want to talk about it. He didn't really talk to her at all anymore.

From what she heard, Keldon had had a fourth surgery and was still in a coma. She didn't know if that was good or bad. His parents didn't allow anyone to visit him. That was probably for the best. The rivalry stuff was stressful to her, so she could only imagine how his parents felt. Their only son's life was changed forever.

15 JOEY MARSHALL

He was only able to see Keldon once. They had been friends since middle school and now his parents thought they couldn't trust him. He didn't blame them.

He had warned Keldon about dating a girl from Heru. Especially one with a nasty attitude like Zandrea. He didn't understand what he saw in her. He knew what she saw in him. He was stable, drama-free and apparently gullible. He knew she had to have something to do with him getting burned up, but he wasn't sure what it was. It was probably a prank that no one saw coming.

Every time he thought about Keldon, all he felt was guilt. Keldon was the only person he knew who didn't participate in school activities. From the first time he had met Keldon in his seventh grade class, he thought he acted like an old man. They first spoke in recess and had been friends since.

"We need another person on our soccer team. Can you play?" He saw him doing homework on the small steps by the football field.

Keldon looked up at him, then looked around to make sure he wasn't talking to anyone else before answering, "Nah, I gotta finish my homework."

Joey looked around the field. The prissy girls were wearing dresses. He knew they didn't want to get dirty. The dorks weren't coordinated enough to run in a straight line. He couldn't ask the eighth grader in the corner. He always wanted to fight someone. Keldon looked like his only viable option. "Why you doing homework at recess?"

"I'm trying to get a head start."

"What you mean? Math homework don't even take long."

"It takes hours. I want to watch TV tonight, but I can't if I still have homework to do." Keldon looked over at the kids waiting for Joey.

"Y'all can play short," he heard one of the kids call to him. "We gotta get started."

"And I don't even like playing soccer." Keldon put his head back down.

"Just play with us for like ten minutes. I'll do your homework for you." Joey wasn't sure how well he played, but his team had no chance of winning if he was short. He just couldn't lose again. No one would want to be on his team if he did.

That got Keldon's attention. "For real?" he asked.

"Yea, man. I'm actually already done with mine so if you want, you can just copy it . Let's go."

After that, Joey helped Keldon with his math homework in exchange for him playing on his team during pickup games. Keldon turned out to be a natural athlete, but that just wasn't his interest. As soon as he was old enough, he was only interested in making money. All of his free time was spent either working a part time job or learning how to code. His plan was to be a software developer when he graduated while attending college on the side. Joey thought that was backwards thinking but never told him.

Joey begged Keldon for months to come to a sports game, any sports game. People were starting to think he was weird because he hardly ever talked to anyone. He was the same quiet, patient, and reserved kid that he met by the football field.

"I never hear you say Keldon's name anymore. Are you guys still friends?" his mom asked one day after he hung out with the swim team.

"We are, but we don't have many things in common. He doesn't even like to hang out."

"You two still like math and those comic book movies," his mom responded.

"That was enough in middle school, but we're in high school now. I go to games and play a sport. He won't even come to a basketball game with me."

"You invited him to a basketball game even though he doesn't like sports?"

"It's high school, Mom. Yes."

"Have you invited him to see you swim?"

"No one comes to swim meets."

"I'm sure he'd rather support a friend than watch random kids yell at each other."

His mom was on to something. He thought Keldon would say no, but he asked him anyway. He was surprised when he actually agreed. He wanted to see Joey swim. He wanted to support his friend. He wished he didn't. Then he wouldn't be fighting for his life. Why was Keldon such a good guy? This made Joey feel guilty again. That swim meet was where he met that stupid bitch from Heru.

He saw them talking when it was time to go. He had never seen him talking to girls before so he didn't want to make it awkward. He waited for the conversation to end before walking up to him. "You know she goes to Heru."

"Yea, I can tell. She was sitting on their side."

"There's plenty of girls at Huey P."

"I know," Keldon laughed. "I go there."

"I'm just saying. You can do better."

"She's cute."

"You know that's not what I'm talking about."

"You guys really take that rivalry thing too far, don't you?"

Joey thought that was the end of it. He went from not talking to girls to meeting up with Zandrea every other day. Joey asked him at school every week if he had broken up with her. He always smiled and shook his head. He had the patience of a snail swimming in molasses and was as calm as a sloth sleeping in a swamp. Joey had never seen him angry. That's why he knew he didn't deserve this. The guilt kept piling on.

Joey couldn't shake the feeling that his friend was being used. Keldon called him one day about a geometry assignment. It was a few weeks before the incident. It wasn't uncommon for Keldon to do that a couple times a year. He was really smart, but he could get lost in concepts. Joey had a gift of making the complex sound simple, especially in math.

Once Joey was sure that Keldon understood the instructions, he switched the subject. He decided to try to force some sense into him one last time. He had been itching to ask him something he had found out a few days before.

"So I see you got an Instagram page."

"Yea. It was Z's idea. It might help us with a project. She set it up for me."

Joey already knew that and that was exactly what he wanted to talk about. "Do you post the pics or does she?"

Keldon laughed. "It's on my phone, but she works it."

Now Joey was sure she was using him. "I bet she has your password too."

"Yea, she does. It's not a big deal. We use each other's computers a lot."

"Did you ever hear of that prank when some girl from Newton got a Falcon to say that he wished he had a Panther girl?

"Nah. I'm not really attentive to those. You know that."

"That makes you a perfect target."

"I like Z. I know you're looking out for me, but you have to give her a chance."

"Just tell me what you see in her. Besides her looks?"

Keldon laughed again. "Well, if you really want to know, she's smart."

"Is she really or is she pretending, just to get next to you?"

"Whoa. I didn't think I was that great of a catch for someone to lie on my behalf." Keldon laughed again. He always laughed. Nothing was a big deal to him.

Joey remembered him saying something about her having a snake.

"So what she has a python!" Joey blurted. "How you like reptiles and you don't even like dogs?" She was turning him into a different person.

Keldon just laughed. "I knew you wouldn't understand. I just like her, that's all. She's good for me."

"Is she there with you now? Cough twice and I'll come save you."

"Seriously. Can you try to give her a chance? We're coming to the football game together."

"What football game?" The question was rhetorical. He already knew it was the Panther vs. Falcon game.

"She wants to help me squash this rivalry thing you guys are always talking about. We actually have a great idea. See… something else we have in common. Can you please try to give her a chance?"

Keldon waited patiently on the other end of the phone. Other than math help, he had never asked Joey for anything. Joey had a list as long as his arm of things he had asked of Keldon. He told him yes, even though he knew it was a lie.

They didn't belong in any particular cliques, but word got around in their small circle that he was dating someone from Heru. It was hard to avoid with having an Instagram page. That was what Joey was afraid of. Keldon wasn't well-known, but those that did know him could think he was a traitor.

Tell ya boy to be careful, he got a text the night before the big game from Ty.

Joey started to write a reply when an image came in. It was a picture of Zandrea. She was at the pre-game hugged up in the corner with some guy wearing Heru colors. Her face was turned away from him, directly in sight of the camera. The guy's arms were wrapped around her. Joey was hot. *Man, I'll try, but he won't listen to me.*

I ain't no snitch, but those falcons can't be trusted.

Ty couldn't have texted more truer words. Joey thought about it all night and the next morning. He wanted to meet up with Keldon before the game, but of course he was busy. When he had finally caught up with him, he was talking to Amaris. She was a nice girl and she had nice friends. It was perfect.

"Where you been, man? I been hitting you up," he asked Keldon when he walked up.

"My bad, bro. I got here a little late and I was supposed to meet up with Z, but she's not answering."

"She's a busy girl," Joey was trying to throw shade, but he knew Keldon wouldn't catch it. "You don't already know Amaris, do you?"

"No, I don't think we've met." She smiled and extended her hand. "It's nice to meet you."

He returned her smile, "The pleasure's all mine." He leaned over and kissed the back of her extended hand.

Smooth, Joey remembered thinking. Keldon looked at his phone before looking around. Joey could tell that he was about to bolt, so he pulled his personalized lighter from his pocket. A pyro trick would hold them for at least a few minutes.

Joey had been playing with fire since he was five. He was punished severely when his dad caught him lighting matches when he was seven, so he learned to hide his interest. But that didn't last long. At age nine, he burned down his family shed while attempting to burn a used paper towel. He still had the burn marks on his hand. He got out in time but didn't realize that the lawn equipment was in there. Lawn equipment that was full of gas. The amount of safety classes he was forced to take should have been enough to deter him from ever setting another fire, but it wasn't.

His uncle caught him that next year, trying to light a fire pit in his backyard. Joey knew it was over for him. His dad had threatened to send him away if he ever touched fire again. He just knew his uncle was going to turn him in, but he was surprisingly calm.

He promised not to tell his dad if he could get him to explain what he liked about the fire. Joey went into grave details, pleading with his uncle not to send him away. His uncle laughed and explained that he had some weird addiction. His uncle was a firefighter and had studied pyromania before. He was confident that with proper care, Joey could be helped. He didn't know what that meant then, but he soon learned.

He learned everything about fire. Different types of fire, the degrees of fire, best methods of acceleration and extinguishment. If he was there when Keldon got burned, he probably could have helped. From his research, he knew that Keldon's case had to be severe.

By middle school, he got into pyro tricks. This was the tool that kept his addiction at bay. He often dreamt of having his own show in Vegas. Being a firefighter, his uncle wasn't afraid and supported his interest. His dad, on the other hand, never let him live down that fire. He encouraged him in a different way. He introduced him to the opposite of fire: competitive swimming.

He and his father used to watch *The Avatar* together. He said something about him being a leader of the Fire Nation, but he'd have more powers if he also mastered the Water Tribe. He thought it sounded dumb until he had a collection of medals. The other bonus was that his parents were no longer afraid that he would burn the house down.

He was losing his best friend and had lost his lighter. The engraved lighter was the last thing his uncle gave him before he died. Joey was feeling enraged. Helpless. Swimming laps wasn't working. He wanted to burn something. He wished that it was him who had burned down that falcon in front of Heru's school.

"Joey," his dad's voice broke his thoughts. He couldn't decide if that was anger or excitement in his voice. His next line helped him decide. "The fire marshal is at the door for you."

16 RON LAIN

Ron always said that the school gave the Black panthers a bad name. What was once a serious Civil Rights group had turned into a school that collected a cadre of cowards. Of all the pranks, the worst one was being played on him. His girl was dating a Panther punk. Ron did feel bad for the guy. No one deserved to get burned up like that, but why would he try to date a Heru girl? He should have known better. He pled with Zandrea over and over again that she didn't need to date that guy. He knew she was trying to get him back.

Ron and Zandrea were a good couple. Some people said she was too smart for him, but he didn't need to be smart. He was an athlete. He made a few little mistakes and she had to be all dramatic and break up with him. He thought she was joking, but she stopped answering his calls and blocked him on Insta. She even ignored him in class.

A few weeks later, it finally sunk in. He was at basketball practice with Third. Third was scrolling on his phone while Ron was taking a sip of water.

"Yooo," Third said. "This yo girl?" He gave his phone to Ron.

She was tagged in a picture with a tall, goofy looking guy wearing a black and gray shirt. "I know this ain't what I think this is?" He clicked on the tagged name. It didn't take long to confirm what he suspected. She was dating a Panther. "Man, whatever. You know I been done with her." He gave the phone back to Third and walked to the court. He was pissed but didn't want to show it.

He didn't want to care about her. He had been dating other girls. She was boring anyway. He told himself that over and over again, but he'd find himself spying on her from one of his other Instagram pages. He went from thinking *He ain't got nothing on me* to thinking *What does she see in him?*

It's not that he cared. Not really. But since he saw her at the pre-game party, he figured he might as well ask. "What's up, Drea?"She was standing around talking to those same two friends of hers.

She looked at him and rolled her eyes.

He smiled at her outfit. It seemed she was finally taking his advice. They wore matching cropped Heru hoodies. She had a nice figure. It was 'bout time she showed it off. "Can I talk to you for a minute?" he asked. Her friends giggled. "Just for a second," he added.

She sighed. Her friends walked away. "We'll be right back, girl."

"What do you want?" she asked.

"I see you switched sides."

She rolled her eyes. "And."

"And, you know that's not a good look. Come on now. It's a disgrace to the school."

"Aren't you one to talk," she huffed. "You think I care about some stupid school rivalry?" She put her hand on her hip. "Is that it?"

"I know you just trying to make me jealous." The cocky role wasn't working. She looked like she would walk away at any moment. He put his arms around her and whispered in her ear, "I'm sorry, okay?"

She stood still. "Can you please get off me?"

"Come on, baby," he whispered. She wrapped her hands around his arms, trying to push him away from her. "Don't you miss me?" he asked.

"Get off of me." She was louder this time. He let her go. She walked away to find her friends. Ron decided that she just wasn't ready yet. He'd give her more time. Rome wasn't built in a day. He knew she'd be at the big game. Her friends had always pressured her to go.

He saw her twice at the game. It had to be fate. Then he finds out her boyfriend gets burned up. If that wasn't a sign, he didn't know what was. Even the universe didn't think they should be together.

The first time he saw her at the game, she was with her crew. It was a few minutes before that stupid fight he almost had with a couple of punks ass Panthers. He told her to drop that chicken dinner and get with a winner. He laughed. It was a corny joke, but he thought she'd at least look his way. She didn't. He and Third were minding their own business talking about how the football team cleaned the field with those Panthers when a Panther decided to jump into their conversation.

"You didn't see your mascot, " one of them said. "Looks like he'd rather be a Panther." Both of the guys laughed. Ron didn't know if they knew about the prank pulled on him or not. He tried not to look offended.

"Yea," Third said. "I bet your girl wanna be a Falcon."

The Panthers laughed. "This the only time y'all can talk trash. I bet y'all won't be saying that in a few months."

"We ain't scared of y'all." Ron balled his fist and took his stance.

One of the guys pushed him hard. He fell back into someone. He was resetting his balance when he saw the shocked look on everyone's face. He should've stole a punch right then, but he turned around to look, too. There were huge yellow bubbles all over the side of the school.

"Let's go, man," Third said. They walked away for two seconds before hearing the sizzle and crackle that was fire.

Ron helped Third drag a few people to the open area next to the school. There were plenty of picnic tables for people to catch their breath. He was about to sit there as well, until he saw Zandrea. He didn't know why, but he smiled when he saw her. When he noticed her walking back toward the fire, he ran to get to her. Something was wrong.

"What are you doing? It's dangerous over there." He grabbed her and pulled her back to the parking lot.

"I can't find him. I'm just trying to see-"

"You don't need to see anything." She was pulling against him. "Let me look at you. Are you hurt? Where are your girls?"

"They're here. Everyone else is here. Let me go." She finally broke free of him.

He thought about following her, but he was in awe to see the front of the whole school in flames. He had never seen anything like it. He must have been running on adrenaline before.

He remembered thinking it was just like the Panthers to host a football game at an unsafe school. He remembered when their principal blasted the superintendent at the school board meeting. That was proof enough that he destroyed his school for the money. Ron was just wondering what was taking them so long to take him to jail.

He watched the entire video of the Panthers' principal disrespecting the school board. They played the entire clip on Channel 8 at 8. He didn't watch the news often but if he did, he made sure to watch Channel 8. A Heru alumni was a news anchor there. The day after it aired, he asked several of his teammates if they had seen it. They were all clueless. This was the second time the clip had made news and no one was paying attention. Ron once wondered what he meant when he said, *by any means necessary.* Now he knew.

The devil image of Mr. Dossani obviously wasn't effective. It was time for a new medium. Ron had a future in media, so he didn't have a problem with helping more people understand the message. He got to work on his computer that very night. He downloaded the entire video and brought it into his video editing software. He only needed 15 seconds and the first two had to be the most important. He got to work.

The video started with the most important line, "My kids will get their school improvements by any means necessary." Ron zoomed in and held the frame on Mr. Dossani's angry face. The next image was from the video he downloaded of the fire. He made sure to edit out the watermark and start the burning building after the foam couldn't be seen anymore.

Then the screen showed video snippets of students running and crying. There were plenty videos of that online. Ron made sure most of the students were in gray and black. He really wanted to drive home the lengths that Mr. Dossani was willing to go to in order to disrespect the district. The final part of his clip were quick millisecond images of the fire and the crying kids with a voiceover of Mr. Dossani repeating, "by any means necessary." Each time, the voice was altered to sound deeper and slower. He was looking for a demonic effect. That idea gave him another.

He found a deep, eerie, sound like one you would hear in a movie when the murderer is on a hunt. He played the sample really low in the background. People felt sound waves. Those were almost more important than the actual image. Ron sat back, proud of himself for his work. He then realized it was missing something else. Most people will have their audio off in school. It needed to be more effective. He made the overall video smaller so that he could add caption right on the video. That way, people would know what was happening without listening. Toward the top of the video, he added the text, *Panthers' Principal wants renovations*. At the bottom of the video in a sharp streak font, he wrote, *by any means necessary*. It was perfect.

Ron exported the video and uploaded it to Instagram from his fake account. He added hashtags from each school. He even threw in a few to describe the rivalry and scandal. He was just about to tap the blue check to post it, but thought of one last hashtag to add, #epicschoolprank.

17 TY ARMSTRONG

Ty rubbed his knuckles. They were still sore from when he fought that Falcon at Ginelle's party. He thought the halftime party was a joke until Ty leaned into his face. His ring cut the guy's jaw, but it also bruised his finger. Tuck teased that he knocked those waves smooth off the guy's head. Ty's laugh was cut short when he thought about Keldon. It wasn't looking too good for him. The updates didn't come in too often but when they did, it was the same.

More surgeries, still in coma. Ty didn't know Keldon well. He hung out with Joey sometimes, and Joey hung out with Keldon sometimes. If it wasn't for Joey, he wouldn't even know who Keldon was. The guy didn't talk unless he was spoken to. When he first met him, he thought he was slow.

He went over to Joey's to play a couple of games and Keldon was there.

"Have you met Keldon?" Joey introduced them.

"Nah. What's up, man," Ty said. Keldon just nodded. They played games for an hour and Keldon didn't open his mouth once. Ty thought it was odd that he had an entire conversation with Joey without so much as a, *yes, okay, cool* or something from Keldon.

Ty decided to start a conversation with him to see what would happen. "Ay man, what school you go to?"

"Huey P," Keldon responded without looking away from the game.

"You play any sports? I hadn't seen you up there. Did you just start?" He was seated, but Ty could tell by his broad shoulders that he should be some type of athlete.

"Nah."

Ty wasn't sure which question he had answered, so he waited a second to see if he would elaborate. He didn't. "Nah you don't play sports, or nah you didn't just start."

"Neither."

"Man of few words?" Ty asked. He couldn't tell if Keldon was being rude. Keldon's player died. He looked over at Ty. He smiled and shrugged.

"You're right, Ty. He is definitely a man of few words. I don't even know how we became friends."

Joey and Keldon shared a glance and a laugh before Keldon started a new game.

They went on like that for a few hours, Joey and Ty talking with nothing much coming from Keldon. Over time, Ty realized that was just how he was. He would see him sometimes in school. If they caught eyes, Keldon would give him a nod, but that was it. For a tall guy, he was easy to miss. Nothing about him stood out and he definitely didn't make his presence known. You could stand right next to him and not even know he was there. That's why Ty was shocked when he received a friend request from him on Instagram.

"Guess who sent me a friend request on IG," he told Joey before swim practice one day.

"That bad ass girl from last week's meet?"

"Pshh. I wish. Nah. Ya boy." Joey looked at him, confused. "Sir don't talk a lot," he said.

Joey laughed. "Don't call my boy that." He shook his head. "That is a clever name, though."

"You think he'd get mad if he heard me call him that?"

"I doubt it, but I don't know. I've known him almost five years and I haven't seen him mad once."

"Maybe he's ready to be social since he's on social media."

Joey chuckled, "That ain't him. That's his girl." Joey shook his head.

"Say what?" Ty pulled his phone from the locker. He went to IG and accepted the friend request. Keldon had ten posts. Three were pictures of a black and white computer screen. Five were of Keldon working on a computer. He didn't face the camera in either of those pictures. Then there were two pictures of him and a girl. They were selfies. He zoomed in. The big eyes, colorful braids, and slender face didn't seem familiar. "I don't think I've seen her before." Ty zoomed in on the second picture. He didn't know why. It was almost the same as the last one.

"That's because she goes to Heru."

Ty's head was still pointed toward his phone, but his eyes darted to Joey. He lifted his head then cocked it to the side. Joey didn't say anything. He just watched his reaction. Ty was not expecting that answer. "You didn't tell ya boy about –"

"Yea, yea man. More than I cared to. I'm officially a hater now. I swear if it was anyone else, I would have been cursed out by now." Joey threw his hands in the air. "I wanted to curse myself out. Like leave the boy alone, but he don't get it. He's not like us."

Ty locked his phone in the locker as they prepared to walk out to the pool. "Is he from here?"

"Second generation Panther, dawg," Joey said slowly. "I think his parents raised him wrong. They say the rivalry is dumb."

"Man," Ty responded.

"I mean it's dumb, but dating a bird?" Joey complained. Ty nodded. He understood. Joey didn't even have to explain. "I mean you can date 'em, but they all on IG hugged up. Like c'mon man."

"Tell him to be careful. That's all I can say." Ty warned him then and although it wasn't his business, he warned him again.

Ty had never seen Zandrea in person but being Keldon's friend on IG, he frequently saw pictures of them together on his feed. He was starting to think maybe love was blind until he went to the game pre party Thursday night. That same girl with those colorful braids in full Heru gear was hugged up on someone from Heru. Ty broke every bro code known to man when he snuck that picture of her. He just couldn't stand to see another Panther being done like that, and not by a Falcon. And not one as innocent as Keldon. The boy didn't even speak.

He never found out if Joey showed him the picture or not. At this point, he wouldn't dare bring up Keldon other than asking how he was doing.

Ty looked at Keldon's last video again. That boy looked like he was so in love. Ty shook his head. His parents should have raised him right. Zandrea looked like she was in love, too. She was a good actress. Ty glanced at a few of the comments. They were pretty harsh.

It was all her fault. They need to draw up charges.

If they're drawing up any charges they need to be against the Panther principal. He sacrificed his own students for renovations.

Ty could tell from the posts that both the Panther school Instagram page and Zandrea's Instagram pages had been deactivated. The rivalry wasn't fun anymore, especially since he couldn't swim or play golf. He didn't know how long this ban could last, but he had to find something to do with all of this new free time.

He saw an evil picture of Mr. Dossani. Someone had photoshopped him into a devil. Ty sighed before reading over a few more comments.

Did y'all see @hotboyron grab her in that fire video? LOL. He want that old thing back.

Ty didn't know why, but he tapped on hotboyron's name. The sports ban had him paying attention to the wrong things. He looked familiar, but Ty didn't know why. He scrolled on his page. Just as he suspected, the fire video was there. He had shared it on his page, but somehow it looked different. Ty almost went back to scrolling when it got close to the end because he had seen the video enough times. Right there, at the end, he saw a guy pulling on a girl. She had those long braids. He only knew of one girl with braids that color. It had to be Zandrea.

Wait a minute, he thought. He went through his pictures to find the one he snuck of Zandrea from the party. It was the same guy. That's why he looked so familiar. Wow. He want that old thing back? Keldon was dating this guy's girl?

He wanted to call Joey, but he knew he shouldn't. He had already broke bro code, this wouldn't help the situation. Ty decided it was best that he didn't. He closed the picture. The Instagram page was still up. He decided to scroll through a few more of @hotboyron's pictures. Something else about him was familiar. He looked at the photo of him from game day. He stood there next to another guy in a Heru letterman. He saw those ugly ass red, blue, and yellow Nikes.

Ty covered his gaped open mouth. This is the guy he was about to fight before the fire started. This is the guy he pushed into the bushes. This guy... just happened to be the boyfriend of the Keldon's girlfriend. Something was definitely fishy.

18 SHERRAY SMITH

Zandrea was depressed. She had to be. She wouldn't answer any of Sherray's calls. All Sherray wanted to do was check on her. She looked at her text messages. She had sent her 35 texts since Saturday and hardly received any replies. Zandrea replied every other day with just two words, *I'm fine.*

Everyone kept asking her how Zandrea was and she didn't know what to tell them. She's good. She's bad. She's upset. She's depressed. She didn't know.

Lena was calling her again. She already knew what she wanted but picked up on the first ring. "Hello?"

"Have you talked to her?"

"No. And I'm guessing that you haven't either."

Lena sighed. "I tried going by her house today."

"What happened?" Sherray was going through the motions now. She was starting to wonder if she and Lena were the ones insane. They kept doing the same thing over and over, expecting a different result.

"The same thing that happened the last two times."

"Of course," Sherray replied.

"We have to do something. What can we do?"

"I don't know. Things are getting really crazy around here."

"I know. Did you know those Panther punks set the falcon on fire?"

"It's all over IG. I hope Keldon makes it. If he dies, this will only get worse."

"I'm afraid to go to school. What if they plant a bomb next?"

"They wouldn't do that."

"How do you know? They just killed Heru."

"They burned an oversized, plastic bird. It wasn't even a good replica. We burned down their school."

Lena gasped, "You don't really believe that, do you?"

"You saw that video. Why were there Falcon colors right before the fire happened? More of their kids were hurt."

"Did you see that video of their principal? With his deep demon voice saying, *by any means necessary.*"

"Yea," Sherray sighed.

"I can't believe you. Whatever is wrong with Zandrea must have rubbed off on you. Don't tell me you're going to bring a secret Panther boyfriend to the next game, too."

"No, but they're just people. Just like us. We hang out with them all the time. We were all having a good time at the party Thursday night. What happened to that energy?"

"If you weren't the one hosting, I wouldn't have even come."

"Didn't I see you hanging with some of the Panthers. You were having fun, too. Everyone was. Other than the different color shirts, everyone seemed to be the same. Like we were one big happy family."

"Well, that was before they embarrassed our mascot."

"We had our mascot at halftime. I don't even think that mascot they had was real. It was a harmless joke."

"I talked to Third. That mascot was real. Luckily, he had just ordered a new one. When they got it back, it was all cut up and stinky. They basically ruined it. It had to be thrown in the trash. Those things are expensive."

"More expensive than replacing a burned school?"

"It's only the front of their school," Lena forced a sigh. "I don't know what has gotten into you. Just let me know if you talk to Zandrea before I do."

"Will do." Sherray heard the beep before she finished talking. She couldn't believe that she hung up on her. Lena was just like everyone else, jumping to conclusions and making up reasons to be mad.

The rivalry was something the students kept up to get themselves excited. To have something to look forward to. No one actually said that, but she knew it to be true. She had hosted quite a few parties, and her older siblings had before her. They bled blue, yellow, and red but they were humans first. What type of humans would destroy other humans because of a stupid idea? There was no real threat. Just people pulling pranks. Yes, some of them were crass and disrespectful, but they were never truly violent. At least they didn't used to be.

Sherray remembered the first Panther prank she had seen. She was in elementary school at the time. She went to a track meet with her parents to watch her sister run. Her sister ran fourth leg in the 4 x 4. They had been there all day waiting for her big race. The finale. And Sherray was tired. She remembered that she was yawning when she heard the crowd going wild. She jumped up to see why they were yelling. Eight guys ran across the field. They were topless, wearing nothing but short tights. Each of them had a letter painted on their backs in black, outlined in gray. The letters spelled PANTHERS.

She talked about that stunt for weeks. Her sister told her if she thought that was cool, just wait until she got to high school. From then on, her sister would tell her about every prank she saw, down to the smallest details. Her brothers continued the tradition when they made it to high school. She begged them to host the school parties so that she could sneak in. Her parents would forbid it if they couldn't keep an eye on her. She was a professional at throwing parties before she had ever reached high school, so it wasn't a surprise that Heru would choose her as a designated party host at least once a year.

No one could question her allegiance to Heru. She knew that was what Lena was trying to do. Maybe she was a bit more understanding because hosting the parties forced her to come in contact with more Panthers than most, but she came from a long line of Falcons. Nothing could make her forget that.

Lena didn't say anything but she had been questioning Zandrea's allegiance to Heru since she started dating Keldon. When Sherray didn't join Lena in talking sense into Zandrea, she questioned her allegiance too. Sherray would understand side-eyeing Keldon if he played basketball or football, or any sport for that matter, but he wasn't like that. He said he wasn't into the rivalry thing and Sherray believed him.

She was there when Zandrea met Keldon. Zandrea came to watch her swim meet. Zandrea waved at her and gave her two thumbs up when she received her medal. Sherray watched Zandrea focus her face back to her tablet that lay on her lap. Sherray was sure that she was working on that stupid program that she liked so much. Keldon walked up behind her. He peered over her shoulder. She turned around to face him and they both started smiling at each other.

By the time Sherray had washed up and changed, Keldon was walking away. "He's cute," Sherray said when she walked up.

Zandrea turned around with a huge smile on her face. "I think I'm in love. Is it too soon?" They both laughed. Zandrea had just broken up with Ron the week before. Sherray hated Ron. Anyone was better than him.

"Why do you keep picking these bums?" Lena accused when they all went out for pedicures.

"Okay, I get why you call Ron a bum, but you don't even know Keldon," Zandrea defended.

"He goes to Huey P. That's all I need to know." Lena rolled her eyes.

"He's nothing like Ron. I can't wait 'til you guys meet him." Zandrea squealed.

"We don't want to meet no Panthers," Lena said. "Right, Sherray?" Sherray didn't respond.

"She's already met him."

"What?" Lena snapped.

"I did not. I just know she met him at my swim meet," Sherray responded.

"And you approve of this?"

Sherray rolled the thought around in her head for a second before shrugging. "I don't know. I mean... he was cute."

"Is that the only standard?"

"Come on, Lena. Where is the rulebook that says that we can only date Heru guys?"

"We bleed..."

"Blue, yellow, and red," Sherray and Zandrea finished the line with her.

"Exactly," Lena said. "You don't have to only date Heru guys, but you cannot date a Panther. It's forbidden." She raised a finger. "Actually, I think it is in the student handbook." The girls all laughed.

Lena didn't say anything else to Zandrea about it, that she knew of, but she often asked Sherray her thoughts about them dating. "Do you really think she likes him?" Lena asked in history class.

"I don't know," Sherray shrugged.

"I overheard Ron say she was just doing it to try to make him jealous. You know... because she found out he was dating that Panther chick. The one with the long, wavy hair and light brown eyes."

Sherray had heard that rumor too. She wanted to believe that Zandrea would tell her if that was the case, but maybe she wouldn't if it was one of those secret society pranks. Zandrea didn't spend a lot of time with them and when she did, she was focused on a tablet or computer. She had been suspecting that for a while. She wouldn't tell Lena though, because she believed all conspiracy theories. She knew the society was real because her sister was in it. Sherray would help her come up with silly pranks to pull. "Yea, I heard that too," she sighed.

"They're all on Instagram together," Lena continued. "She's tagging him in her pictures. Everyone can see that."

"Maybe it is to make Ron jealous, but I'm pretty sure she's over him."

"I know you're busy with the party tonight, so let's ask her tomorrow. At the game." Lena really thought she was a detective.

"Why does it matter?" Sherray asked.

"It's not good for her reputation."

That was it. Sherray knew she wasn't worried about Zandrea's reputation. She was worried about her own reputation. Guilty by association. She still hadn't gotten over that kiss at the basketball game two years before. For no reason at all, Lena was still trying to prove her school loyalty.

"Think about it. Pretty soon, the football team is going to stop endorsing your parties because they'll think you favor the Panthers."

She turned to look at Lena. Was she serious? Wait, could that happen? These athletes seemed to be way too vested in this rivalry thing. Especially the football players. If she didn't have the endorsement of the football team, she didn't have a party. And if she didn't have a party, her popularity could be erased overnight. Instead of party girl, she could turn into *what's her face who used to have parties*. She was the youngest in her family. She was basically carrying the legacy of a record-breaking track star, a varsity football captain, and a varsity basketball captain. She was an athlete, too. A swimmer, but she wasn't even the best swimmer. She wasn't even second best. Those parties were her reputation. Her brother would never live it down if she lost the party hosting rights.

"You know Natasha's parents just bought Lebron's old house. I've already heard people talk about how nice it would be to party in that house."

Sherray sighed, "What do you want me to do?"

"Just have my back this time. Don't do that," Lena waved her hand in front of her, "thing you do. Playing devil's advocate."

"Huh," Sherray was in awe. "Okay," she agreed.

Friday night started all wrong. First, Zandrea didn't show up until the top of the second quarter. Second, her phone was dead as usual, so it took them forever to find her. And third, they didn't know what the hell she was wearing. Seeing the twin attire gave Sherray pause. Did they really have on matching sweaters? Maybe Zandrea's allegiance had changed.

They tried to play it cool when they finally found her hugged up with Keldon. "Heeey," Sherray said when they got near. The pitch was too high and the greeting was too long, but she tried to mask it.

"We have been looking for you," Lena declared.

"I know. I'm sorry, guys. The mailman was late and my freaking phone died."

A ringing phone caused everyone to look to Keldon. He looked down at his phone before looking back up to meet their eyes. "It's my mom.

I'll call her back," he smiled.

"We're missing the whole game. If we don't hurry, we'll miss halftime," Lena complained.

"Umm… yea guys, about that. I'm sitting with Keldon and he wants to sit on the Panthers' side."

"What!" Lena exclaimed.

"Oh," Sherray sighed.

"I need to call my mom back. Why don't you go with your girls to the Heru side and just meet me at the fence after halftime? We can watch the rest of the game on the Panthers' side. Is that cool?"

"No-" Lena started, but Sherray pulled her arm.

"Thanks, babe." Zandrea kissed him on the cheek. "See you in a bit. Don't be late. Remember, I don't have my phone." Lena grabbed Zandrea's arm and started walking toward the game. Sherray was right behind them.

"I'll be right there waiting. You had me at hello world." Zandrea blew Keldon a kiss.

"What is up with you? What are you guys wearing?" Lena was still pulling Zandrea, but she didn't seem to mind.

"He's so sweet, isn't he?" Zandrea looked at Sherray. Lena's death stare told her not to respond to that question.

"What is up with you and that Panther?" Lena finally asked.

"Um… he's my boyfriend, but you already know that, so… where are you going with this?"

Lena looked to Sherray. She knew that it was her turn. "Is this a phase, a genuine connection, or…" Sherray couldn't believe she was asking Zandrea the question, but she did. "Are you just doing this to make Ron jealous?"

Zandrea stopped walking in her tracks. She looked from Sherray to Lena, then back to Sherray. Sherray immediately wished that she could take that question back. Why did she even listen to Lena? The sound of a wounded lion brought Sherray back to her senses. She walked toward Zandrea. "I'm sorry," she pled. Lena huffed behind her.

"You know what, guys? I think I'll just wait by the fence," Zandrea stood directly in front of Lena. "for my boyfriend," she boasted before storming off.

That was the last time they talked to Zandrea. They hadn't seen her since.

19 JESSE JACKSON III

That last stunt caused the superintendent to require 24-hour surveillance around Huey P. and Heru High. The news stations had flipped the script and were now hating on both schools. *What's going on in Education? Have our High Schools Gone Mad,* were just some of the headlines. To make matters worse, the athletes were considering transferring out of Heru en masse. School wasn't school without the sports. Maybe they did take it too far. Jesse corrected his thought, the Panthers took it too far. They always took it too far. They couldn't settle on the fact that they were the lesser school. Jesse would have to double time on Zandrea's app project. If he was instrumental in doing something to bring the schools together, it would improve the legacy. No stress, and his dad could finally get off his back. Maybe even fix his mistakes.

Jesse didn't like being around stress. He took the district's offer for excused absences and convinced his parents to let him spend the week at their timeshare. His dad quickly agreed, afraid that any association with the fire would affect their legacy. He was always concerned about legacy. Jesse only heard about the stress of the rivalry when he answered calls from his teammates. That was all they talked about, so he didn't take their calls often.

"What's up, Darryl," he answered his phone.

"What's up, Third. When you going back to school?"

"When they make me."

"You're missing out, man."

"Did sports come back? I'll leave right now."

Darryl laughed. "Naw, man. I'm just teasing. It's boring as hell. I wish I had options like you."

"I bet you do," Jesse changed the subject. "I already heard yo lame ass school burning our falcon. Anything else happen since I've been away?"

Jesse and Darryl were cousins, but they used to be like best friends, but that relationship was slowly slipping away. It didn't help that his aunt married a Panther who insisted, almost forced Darryl to go to Huey P. The rivalry hadn't affected them before but after that halftime stunt, Jesse really didn't trust him. It couldn't be a coincidence that a week after Jesse insulted the Panthers' tired mascot costume and bragged on the new falcon his dad bought for Heru, the old costume appeared at the halftime show.

"I think you about summed it up." Darryl was quiet for a moment. Jesse figured he was thinking. "There's a few rumors, but I know you don't want to hear those."

Darryl was right. Jesse made sure anyone he talked to stuck to the facts. It wasn't that he didn't want to know, but he preferred to keep his anxiety down. He knew his dad started the society and he didn't want anything leading back to either of them. Rumors caused unnecessary worry. One of his middle school basketball coaches taught him a trick that he had learned from his therapist.

"Do you like lemonade?" his coach had asked him. Jesse was confused about the unrelated topic. His coach quickly explained that situations could be sour, but only he had the power to decide how to deal with it. Jesse had been making lemonade out of lemons ever since.

He could sit at school, listen to rumors, worry that someone may blame him, which could cause him to lose his chance of playing Heru basketball; or he could take the excused absence, relax, and take a vacation for a week. He hadn't had a panic attack since he learned how to make lemonade and he planned to keep it that way.

"Well, I was just checking on you, man."

"I'm good," Jesse replied. "I'll holla at you when I get back in town." He ended the call.

Jesse liked to take the high road, until those stupid pranks landed on him. His sophomore year, he dated the prettiest cheerleader in school. She looked better than a model. They were the perfect couple until a stupid Panther prank pulled them apart. Why would he continue to date a chick that was kissed by a Panther, right in front of both schools? No explanation necessary. He was done right then.

His dad wanted him to be more involved with boosting the image of the school. It was his legacy, he said. Jesse just wanted to play basketball. His dad continuously tried to prove to his grandfather that he didn't curse the school. That he didn't destroy the pristine image of Heru that his grandfather helped build. Jesse didn't really care about any of that.

All Heru students knew that his dad, Jesse Jr., pulled strings behind the curtains. He was never at the school, but his dad was the one who had handpicked the principal. He was the one who decided the retired NBA player should be their next basketball coach. He was the one who chose the superintendent. He said it was their legacy as Heru men. Jesse was a third generation Falcon.

His great grandfather, Jesse Sr. was amongst the men who chose to name the school after the ancient god. His grandfather was a prominent basketball and football player when the school was first built. His father was also a star football player, but his senior year was the turning point for the school. It was what marked, as his grandfather put it, the Heru curse.

His dad was the wide receiver who failed to catch the flailing balls that the superintendent had thrown. Afterward, they started losing more games in more sports than they had ever before. Jesse believed that this was what prompted his dad to start the society. His dad never mentioned the society, but he often told Jesse to keep an ear out if any student needed help upholding the Heru image. That's what he said, but what he meant was destroying the Panther image. No one told him anything and he didn't want to know anything, but everyone knew who his dad was, and he'd given his personal number to a few students who had asked. He hoped this latest prank wasn't one that he was indirectly involved in. His dad swore he didn't know anything about it, but Jesse didn't know if he believed him.

No matter how much Jesse tried to stay out of trouble, trouble always found him. It was like game day when he and Ron were minding their own business, laughing at how horrible the Panthers were again, when the Panther fans just had to jump in it. He was just about to tell Ron that a guy had on that same ugly ass sweater his girl had on.

The guy was walking toward them. He was holding his phone up to his ear when he stopped to pick something up. That sweater had the school colors of both schools. Ugh, the colors didn't even look good together. He turned to Ron, right when the Panthers walked up to them.

"You didn't see your mascot, " one of them said. "Looks like he'd rather be a Panther," the Panthers laughed.

"Yea," Jesse said. "I bet your girl wanna be a Falcon."

"I bet y'all won't be saying that in a few months," one of the Panthers accused.

"We ain't scared of y'all." Ron was always ready to start a fight and this day was no different.

Jesse thought he heard a cat screech when one of the Panthers pushed Ron hard. He fell back into the guy with the ugly sweater, who fell right into the bushes. The ugly sweater was uglier from behind. After the guy pulled himself out of the bushes, Jesse saw that the entire back of the sweater was a fuzzy yellow. Jesse was wondering which team he came to support when he noticed a frightened look on everyone's face. He followed their gaze to see foam covering the bushes and up the side of the school. By the time he turned back around, the bushes were on fire. Some people were a lot closer to the bushes than he was. He saw a Panther cowering like a baby near him. He went to pull him out the way as someone came to help. A group of them tried to help as many people as they could.

It was a day he'd rather forget and he was doing a pretty good job of it too. He deactivated his IG that night. He didn't know if his dad had something to do with it but if he did, he didn't want to be around to find out. His dad was sneaky. He knew that he had arranged a meeting with the superintendent and the school principal. That happened to be the same night the falcon was burned. Something fishy was happening, but Jesse forced himself not to speculate.

Would his dad really start a fire? Jesse didn't know what to believe. He didn't want to believe anything.

20 ZANDREA EVANS

Zandrea felt horrible. Everything went bad, and fast. She should have known she wasn't worthy of being happy for long. Life never worked out like that for her. Was it too much to want it all? Great grades, the perfect boyfriend, popularity, and to save the world. Sometimes, she wished she could go to sleep at night and wake up with that perfect life. Every time things started looking up, they pivoted fast.

Zandrea was always smart. She lived on the honor roll. She had the perfect friends. They were pretty, kind, and supportive. One of them was Mrs. popular herself, a Heru legacy, which made Zandrea popular by association. Then she started dating Ron. He was a double athlete and relatively popular. Things were looking up, until her life did a 180.

It started with Ron. He never was the perfect boyfriend, but Zandrea was fine with overlooking some things. She thought he loved her, but he kept wanting her to change. She was making him look bad when they were around friends because she explained things he didn't understand. She didn't try to embarrass him. She thought when people asked a question, they wanted to know the answer. If it had anything remotely to do with academics, nine times out of ten, she knew the answer. She learned to say things such as, *I don't know* and *I'm not sure.* It stung at first, but she got used to it.

Then he told her she should probably change her wardrobe too, and to see if she could borrow some of Sherray's clothes. Lena and Sherray wore a uniform of cropped shirts with legs on display religiously. Her graphic tees and jeans were boring. Her friends always dressed so nice. He would want to take her out more if she didn't always wear those weird T-shirts that no one understood. She casually asked Sherray if she could borrow some of her clothes but when she wore them, he didn't even notice. She noticed when she stopped coding, but she didn't realize then that her grades were starting to slip. She was spending so much time worrying about what Ron wanted and what he would think that she wasn't paying attention to her assignments and their due dates. Even when she knew she had an assignment due, she would find her mind drifting while trying to do her work.

She let all that slide, but finally drew the line when she found Ron was dating someone from Huey P. She had just got off the phone with him. He thought he had hung up, but he hadn't. She knew that she shouldn't have listened, but she couldn't help herself. Ron said he was hanging out with the guys, but he was saying that a lot lately.

She hardly saw him anymore outside of the one class they shared.

"Do I hear wedding bells soon," Third joked. She was relieved to hear a familiar voice. Maybe he was just hanging with his friends. She reached to hang the phone up.

"Hell naw," Ron bragged. Zandrea didn't like the sound of that.

"Whatever happened to that girl you were talking to from Huey P.?" another guy asked.

"She's finally ready to meet up with me," Ron answered. "I'm going to see her when I leave here." Zandrea knew then that she was going to listen as long as she could and was happy she did.

Ron apparently had a few girlfriends. He didn't even consider them girlfriends really. Apparently, she was just his friend. His friend that he wanted to dress, talk, and act a certain way. It made sense why he didn't like taking pictures together or tagging each other online. Simple things that most couples do. He always found an excuse. She listened to everything. It took twenty minutes for him to realize that his phone was still on.

"Hello?" he said.

"It's over," she hung up.

She called her friends crying. They all talked together on three-way. They were relieved that she had broken up with him. Apparently, neither of them liked him, but they didn't want to say anything. She was mad at them for that. She made them promise to never hold their tongues about her relationships again. Now that she thought about it, that must've been why they confronted her at the game.

She missed Keldon so bad. To make matters worse, she didn't even get to visit him. His parents hated her. It made sense to hate her now, but they had always hated her. She didn't understand why.

The first time she visited his house, she noticed it. They sat in the dining room, side by side. Their laptops were almost touching. She was entering a really long code when his mom walked in. She didn't even notice that she had.

"Z, this is my mom," she had heard Keldon say.

"Okay. Wait a minute. I'm almost done," she replied. She didn't want to lose her concentration. It took her a few moments, but she was finally done. She smiled and raised her hand. "Finished!" she announced. "Now, what were you saying?" she asked.

Keldon smiled and shook his head. "I was going to have you meet my mom, but I guess you'll have to do that later. Now let's see if it works."

She was obsessed with programming and had somehow found her soulmate at, of all places, a swim meet. She was studying a Python lesson on her tablet while waiting for Sherray. He walked up behind her. "You had me at hello world," he whispered in her ear.

She turned around with a smile. She didn't know if he understood the reference or had simply read her shirt from across the swimming pool. It was super cheesy, but the simple phrase could help her spot another programmer more than any conversation could.

"Is that Python you're studying?" he asked. He had seen her tablet.

She knew then that he did understand her shirt. Her heart fluttered. She stood to greet him. "Yes, it is."

"You must be brilliant," he said. "Here I am, still studying C++."

"No. I just happened upon it." It's not what she wanted to say, but she didn't want to scare him off. She mastered HTML in elementary. She devoured C++ in middle school. She still used both, but added Python a few years before when she realized she had an interest in computational nuclear engineering. She no longer explained that to people. She didn't like the look they gave her when she tried. Every question they would ask would send her rambling and they would get bored. She hid that she was a programmer in plain sight.

"You're being modest." His smile widened. He had the most beautiful dimples she had ever seen.

She looked away. She knew she was blushing. She saw Sherray walk into the locker room. That meant that she might have a few minutes.

"It's okay." He stretched his neck to her until his eyes, peering over his glasses, met hers. She turned to face him. "Maybe you can tell me more about it over coffee, or sodas, or milkshakes. Or whatever kind of non-alcoholic beverage you like to drink.

She wanted to tell him that she loved milkshakes, but she didn't want to talk too much. She didn't want him to find a reason not to talk to her. They exchanged numbers.

"Is it okay if I call you this evening?" he asked.

She blushed again. She remembered when she had first given Ron her phone number. He told her he'd call, but he never said that it would take a week. He would see her at school that week and act like she wasn't waiting on his call. "That's perfect," she said.

He looked over his shoulder. His friend was waiting for him. That was her first time seeing Joey. The gray and black was undeniable. That was when she realized that Keldon possibly went to Huey P. *Please, please, please don't let that be an issue.* She thought about that over and over again throughout the day. She was elated to find out that it wasn't.

He called her that evening, just like he said he would. "So…" she started, "You know I go to Heru High," she said.

"That's a good look. I go to Huey P."

She listened for a joke, sarcasm, or objection. Nothing came. "You don't think that would be a problem, do you?"

"Maybe a little bit," he said.

Her voice dropped. "Really?"

"But I don't have to see you every day. The weekends are cool."

She laughed. He laughed too. "You know what I mean. The rivalry stuff."

"I don't care about that," he dismissed. "So tell me about this Python? How long have you been studying it?"

He was seriously interested in what she thought. From that first conversation and every conversation afterward, he made her feel like everything she said was the most important thing to hear in the world. She tried to give him vague answers, thinking he was just making conversation, but he would probe until she elaborated. He never interrupted her even when she would ramble, something she forgot that she could do. She would often apologize for getting off on a tangent and he would remind her not to.

He scared her. He was too perfect. What if this was a prank? Was this the type of prank someone would pull? She had never been in love before, but she was pretty sure that was what it felt like. She decided that she didn't care if it was a prank. She would enjoy his company as long as it lasted. She knew that good things couldn't last forever. Some other girl could figure out how awesome he was. They could go to separate colleges in different states. A lot of things could happen, but she never imagined this.

After a few late night conversations, they realized they were missing important study time. It would be easier if they started studying together. They were so lost in each other that they didn't realize how much everyone hated them together. She told him that Lena had been hassling her about their relationship. She couldn't believe she was making it as big of a deal as she was. That's when he shared that Joey mentioned more times than he could count that they shouldn't be together. His mom even thought they were spending too much time together. How could people hate on two people in love? She didn't understand it. It bothered her and he could tell.

"Are we going to waste energy on things we can't control or use that energy to figure out this program?" he had asked.

She knew he was right. He had a great idea for a new program. He had been working on it for over a year and wanted her help. It could take years to work out the kinks, but they didn't care. They were focused. She had never worked on anything that massive. The fact that he was even trying intrigued her. What if it never worked? What if all that time was wasted? He knew the consequences and he didn't care.

She told him they could cheat. She had moonlit as an ethical hacker a few times. She thought maybe he had known about her work, when she helped a guy trip the basketball scoreboard. Chey swore he didn't use her skills for evil, but she knew better. Keldon was clueless. She smiled. He was in the same world as her, with a school consumed by a supposed rivalry, and he was oblivious to it all.

"I'm pretty sure I can hack into a few social media programs. Just to take a peek. See how the pros do it."

"Sounds good."

She couldn't believe that she had told him she would do that. If anything went wrong, he could testify against her. Only a handful of people knew that she was a hacker. Not even her friends knew. She really hoped that slip wouldn't come back to bite her.

His plan that became their plan was to create a social app that rewarded strangers working together as a team. Their schools would be the perfect focus group. Without giving him too much detail, she got support from Third. People would take the app seriously if she got his support. She told Keldon if they were going to create a social system, he would have to get to know how to use one. He had no type of presence online. He allowed her to set up his IG, but he had only used it once. She did most of the posting. She had to make him request friends.

In the middle of one of their working sessions, her computer died. She had mistakenly left her charger at home. She figured the small break of grabbing his extra charger and rebooting her system would be the perfect time to ask him the question. "Are you going to the game Friday?" He continued to work frantically on his computer.

"I hadn't planned on it."

"Would you go with me?"

"I'll think about it."

"I have a crazy idea. Hear me out."

"I'm listening." Facing the computer, he continued typing.

"I found this website online that can make custom sweaters in any color combination. What if we wore matching sweaters to the game? We can get them in all of our school colors."

He continued to type. She couldn't tell if he liked the idea or not. She was really nervous to even present it to him. She once mentioned to Ron that they should wear the same school T-shirt on the same day and he acted like she asked for his left lung.

"You don't like it?" She sulked in her seat.

"It sounds tacky." He was still typing.

"I know the colors don't look well together, but I was just thinking-You know what? Nevermind."

"You should continue your thought." He sounded reassuring, although he didn't look at her.

She forgot that he didn't like when she second-guessed herself. "Our schools take this rivalry thing too far. I thought we could be an example. That good things can happen when you put the rivalry thing behind you," she cried.

"What happened to your voice?"

She lost her confidence and he noticed. He noticed everything. "You're right. It's probably not a good idea."

"I never said that."

"You don't like the idea."

"All I said was that it sounds tacky, and you agreed."

She rolled her eyes. He was like her, but worse. She now realized why small talk was important. If the only time you spoke was to say what you really thought, that would leave no personality. The connection would be lost. She had to remember that he was nothing like her friends. He actually answered questions, not made facial expressions. The only way to truly know what he thought about anything was to ask him a direct question. Not a similar question. Not a vague question. The actual question that she wanted the answer to.

"Will you wear matching tacky sweaters with me to the Heru vs. Panthers game next Friday?"

He finally stopped typing. He turned to face her. He looked into her eyes for a few seconds, then showed her his lovely dimples. "Of course I will. You had me at hello world."

She lightly punched him in his arm. "You scared me," she laughed.

"I told you I had to think about it."

"What was it that convinced you?"

"You saved us like three months with your hacking trick. You've earned yourself all of the tacky dates you want for the next few weeks."

"But you said I saved us three months."

He turned back to his computer and started typing. She did the same, but made sure to order their sweaters first. They even came with free matching gloves.

Everything went wrong the day of the game. Her sweater shipment was scheduled to come in that morning, but it never came. She was on the phone half the morning trying to track the sweaters down. The Heru vs Panthers game was only once a year. They had to wear the sweaters that day. She promised Keldon that she would track them down and get to the game on time. She didn't.

When she finally got there, he wasn't where they were supposed to meet. She wasn't completely surprised. She was later than she had planned, and the fiasco with the shipping carrier killed her battery and made her forget her charger. She had finally found him, leaning over to kiss some girl's hand, and clearly the girl went to Huey P. Joey was there too. She remembered what Keldon said about Joey not liking them together. She was pissed. She didn't try to hide her anger when Keldon told that girl that it was nice to meet her.

"Are you dating her too?" she accused. Keldon smiled and shook his head. "Well, who is she?"

"Joey said her name was Amaris."

He wasn't going to argue with her. He just watched her with that dumb smile of his. His eyes locked on hers and they never let go. The concern in his eyes caressed the chaos in hers. "Busy day, huh?"

She sighed. It was a busy day. She just wanted them to hang out together, where everyone could see.

"The sweater looks good on you," he said. She was so frustrated that she had forgotten what she was supposed to do. She pulled her bag from her shoulder and took out his sweater and matching gloves. He put the sweater on over his black and gray shirt, then tucked the gloves into his pocket. "It's perfect," he said.

"Let's take a pic."

She waited for him to pull his phone from his back pocket. It was already in selfie mode, probably from the last time she had taken their picture. He pushed a button and held the phone up so that they could smile at it.

"It's on video, silly, not a photo."

Her friends came up after that. She was so close to having a good day. She had pictured the perfect date since the moment he said he'd go to the game and now it was all ruined. That was the last time she saw him. She wanted so desperately to see his face. To hear his voice.

She grabbed the computer. Coding was the only thing that could help her take her mind from it. Just think of how excited he would be if he came out of the coma to find their app working. Her computer was dead. She forgot to charge it.

She went to her computer bag across the room to look for the charger. It wasn't there, but her backup computer was. She and Keldon would go back and forth between her computers and his when they were trying to program and research at the same time. Toggling between tabs wasted precious time. She wanted to see his face. She needed to hear his voice. Anything he could say would drown out the rumors she heard from others.

She clicked on the Google icon then on the apps logo. She would look at their last video again. Hopefully this time, instead of making her cry, it would give her the strength to do the programming for him. It was the last image she saved to her photo gallery.

She had looked at the same video about a million times and it usually sat at the top left of the screen, but there was another video there from the same day. This one, she hadn't seen before. She clicked on it.

It was Keldon. She almost shed a joyful tear to see a candid video of him. She covered her mouth as she watched the shaky screen. The phone fell to the ground. He had on their matching sweater, but he had also put on the gloves she left him. She watched as he opened a zippo lighter, pushed the button, then attempted to touch the flame. The small glow in his hand quickly illuminated him and everything behind him. The video ended within seconds. Zandrea gasped.

Her heartbeat increased. She could not inhale enough air. She stood and paced around the room. She wanted to think, but she couldn't. She had just watched her boyfriend turn into a human fireball. She moved her hand from her mouth and put them on her head. She kept pacing. He had to be in so much pain. She was so optimistic. She never saw him in the hospital, but she just imagined that he would pull through. After watching that video, it was impossible. There was no way. His body started the fire that engulfed the front of their entire school.

She couldn't see. She was hyperventilating.

"Zandrea? Zandrea!" Someone outside was calling her name. Why would someone outside call her name? Where did her room go?

"Zandrea! Zandrea!" The room was shaking. No, she was being shaken.

What if he was already gone and his stupid parents didn't tell her? What happens when people die in the hospital? How would she be notified?

"Zandrea. What's wrong? Sit down." It was her mom's voice. She felt her holding her hands.

"Breathe. Breathe." She could hear her mom taking large breaths. She mimicked her. Inhale. 1.2.3.4.5. Exhale. 1.2.3.4.5. She blinked until she could see her. She was standing right in front of her. She was still in her room.

"Is everything okay? You left your phone in the living room. I came to bring it to you. It was ringing over and over again."

Zandrea didn't care about her phone. She knew it was either Lena or Sherray. She didn't want to talk to them. She didn't want to talk to anyone. She sat on her bed, still trying to catch her breath.

Her mom was smiling. Good for her. Her world wasn't just turned upside down. Her heart wasn't just ripped from her chest.

"It's really good news, baby." Her mom took her phone from the edge of the bed and set it in her lap. "Say hello."

She was annoyed, but she did as her mom asked. "Hello?" She listened and waited for a response.

It was raspy, but it was clear. His voice was music to her ears. "You had me at hello world." It was Keldon smiling through the phone.

What did you think? See what others thought and add your comments in our virtual library at www.cjkpublishing.com/library

Don't stop there. CJK Publishing has engaging stories for the entire family.

Greatest Hall of Fame

Inspire youth with this beginner chapter book series. Read along as the main character, Braxton, is encouraged to reach his goals by seeing the strength of historical figures. All within the Greatest Hall of Fame. Reading level: ages 7-9. Available in print, e-book and audiobook format.

Demarcus Jones and the Solar Calendar intertwines historical facts with current events. The book series helps youth understand the plight of the African Diaspora through the adventures of a pre-teen. Reading level: ages 9 – 12. Available in print, e-book and audio-book formats.

Innovative Inner G's is a variety book that celebrates Black excellence. The coloring pages, lists, games, mazes and more are fun for the entire family. Appropriate for all ages.

When tragedy occurs, everyone claims to know what happened, but there's only one truth. Each book in the 20 People's Lies Book series begins with the facts of the disaster, with multiple witnesses to follow. Do you think you can uncover the truth before time runs out? Appropriate for ages 14+

Our subscribers are a part of every new release. Join us by visiting www.cjkpublishing.com/subscribe

#epicschoolprank